# COMPASSIONATE LOVE

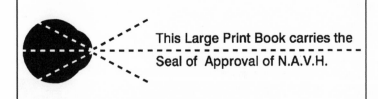

This Large Print Book carries the
Seal of Approval of N.A.V.H.

# COMPASSIONATE LOVE

## THE LEGACY OF FAITH AND LOVE CONTINUES

## ANN BELL

**THORNDIKE PRESS**

*An imprint of Thomson Gale, a part of The Thomson Corporation*

**THOMSON**

™

**GALE**

Detroit • New York • San Francisco • New Haven, Conn. • Waterville, Maine • London

**LIBRARY OF CONGRESS CATALOGING-IN-PUBLICATION DATA**

Bell, Ann, 1945–
    Compassionate love : the legacy of faith and love continues / by Ann Bell.
      p. cm. — (Montana skies ; #2) (Thorndike Press large print candlelight.)
    ISBN-13: 978-0-7862-9245-5 (alk. paper)
    ISBN-10: 0-7862-9245-8 (alk. paper)
    1. Montana — Fiction. 2. Large type books. I. Title.
PS3602.E645425C65 2007
813'.6—dc22                                  2006035369

Published in 2007 by arrangement with Barbour Publishing, Inc.

Printed in the United States of America on permanent paper
10 9 8 7 6 5 4 3 2 1

Dedicated to the caring people of
Montana
who have devoted their lives to
comforting victims of violent crime.

Dedicated to Rev. Eugene Juergensen
of Billings, Montana, whose
compassionate ministry
to the intergenerational needs of the
people
of Montana served as an
encouragement and model
in writing "The Rocky Bluff
Chronicles."
Rocky Bluff is not merely in Montana,
but anywhere love and understanding
are fostered between generations.

# CHAPTER 1

At midnight, Teresa Lennon closed the door of the Rocky Bluff Spouse Abuse Shelter. She had spent the last few hours comforting a distraught, battered young woman, and Teresa sighed now, exhausted. She had finally calmed the troubled woman, then led her to a bedroom on the second floor of the shelter and stayed with her until the woman was ready to sleep. Now Teresa could at last go home.

Teresa had devoted all her working years to helping women in distress, and each person's pain triggered a sense of personal responsibility inside her. She knew what it was like to be emotionally and physically abused. Years before, others had helped her, and now she was always ready to help someone else in crisis. Still, each session left Teresa emotionally drained, and tonight was no different. She lifted her face to the cool fall wind that whirled around her, then made her way to her car.

When she reached her home, she slipped into a nightgown and fell across her bed. Within minutes, she drifted into a deep sleep. Only two hours later, the sharp ring of the telephone pierced the silence of Teresa's bedroom. She grabbed the phone.

"Teresa . . . Teresa," a panicky voice cried. "Can you help me?"

Teresa jerked upright and threw her legs over the side of the bed. As director of the shelter, she was used to being awakened in the middle of the night, and now she was instantly alert.

"I'll do what I can," Teresa said calmly. "To whom am I talking?"

"This is Dawn . . . Dawn Harkness," the voice sobbed. "I can't get ahold of my parents, and I don't know what to do."

Teresa pictured the beautiful daughter of one of the community's leading citizens; Dawn was also the granddaughter of a dear friend. Teresa had not seen Dawn since the younger woman had left for college several months before, and now Teresa felt a wave of concern.

"Dawn, where are you?"

"I'm in the Chief Joseph County Jail," the young coed sobbed.

"Jail? What are you doing there?" Teresa gasped.

"A bunch of us from the college went to a ranch outside of Nez Percé . . . just to have a good time. The police busted the party, and several of us were arrested for using drugs. They won't let us go until we appear with our parents and an attorney. But I'm not able to contact my parents." Dawn gulped back another sob.

"Do you know where they are?" Teresa tried to speak in a calm, relaxed tone even though her heart was beginning to race.

"They're on vacation in the Caribbean. They're not going to be home for a couple of weeks. My brother Jay and his wife Angie are with them too." Her sobs turned to desperation. "I don't know what to do."

"I know it's tough," Teresa replied calmly. "Since you're not able to go any place, try to get some rest tonight. I'll get in touch with an attorney first thing in the morning, and we'll leave immediately for Nez Percé. In the meantime, I'll be praying."

"Thanks," Dawn murmured. "I knew you wouldn't let me down."

Teresa hung up the phone and lay back on her pillow, but sleep escaped her. She thought about the dramatic string of events that had brought her life together with the attractive coed now sitting in the Chief Joseph County Jail.

After an abusive marriage and a traumatic divorce, Teresa had obtained a master's in psychiatric social work from the University of Montana; she had then taken the job in Rocky Bluff, Montana, as director of the Spouse Abuse Shelter. The last fifteen years had been good to her. She had fulfilled a vital need in the community and had made many long-lasting friends, including Dawn's grandmother, Edith Dutton. Teresa had watched Dawn grow from a blond, giggly toddler to a vivacious teenager who anxiously sought the independence of college life. She was aware of Dawn's excessive partying during her senior year in high school, but she had never suspected it would lead to this.

Though Teresa had had less than four hours of sleep, before seven o'clock she was up, showered, and dressed. She dropped two pieces of bread into the toaster, while she dialed an attorney friend, David Wood.

"Good morning." The male voice sounded sleepy.

"Good morning, Dave," Teresa replied. "I'm sorry to call so early, but a crisis occurred last night, and I need immediate legal help."

"I'll do what I can," the young private attorney replied. "What happened?"

"Dawn Harkness called about two o'clock this morning. It seems that a bunch of college kids went to Nez Percé to party. Before the evening was over, the police came and arrested six of them for using drugs. She's now in the Chief Joseph County Jail until her parents and attorney appear before the court. The problem is the Harknesses are vacationing in the Caribbean and won't be back for a couple of weeks. I told her I'd find her legal counsel and drive to Nez Percé first thing this morning. Would you be willing to come with me?"

David paused a moment as he tried to recall the coming day's appointments. "I have a light agenda today." He reached for his robe. "I'd be glad to go with you. The Harknesses have done a lot to support me throughout the years. It's the least I can do. I'll call my secretary and have her reschedule my clients. Give me an hour, and I'll come by and get you."

"Thanks, Dave. I knew I could count on you."

Teresa hung up the phone and took a deep breath. *As much as I hate to, I think I better call Edith. She'd be crushed if one of her fam-*

13

*ily members was in trouble and she wasn't notified so she could pray. Her health has been so bad lately, prayer is the only thing she can do to help her family and friends.*

Teresa dialed the familiar number and waited six rings. "Hello," a breathy voice greeted.

"Hello, Edith. How are you today?"

Recognizing her friend's voice, Edith smiled. "Hi, Teresa. I'm doing fine. I just wish I could get out of the house more often. I miss helping all my friends and family."

"Your prayer power is the best help you can give," Teresa replied. She took a deep breath before continuing. "Please pray for Dawn today. She needs all the support she can get."

Edith's brow wrinkled as she pictured her vivacious granddaughter. "What happened to my sweetie?"

"I hate to be the bearer of bad news," Teresa said. "Dawn called me last night from the Chief Joseph County Jail."

"What was she doing there?" Edith gasped.

"She'd been at a party. The police came by, and she and several other college kids were arrested for using drugs. They won't

14

release her until her parents and attorney appear before the court."

"But Bob and Nancy won't be back from vacation for two weeks," Edith protested.

"That's why she's so upset," Teresa explained. "Her family has always been there to help her, and now she's on her own. She was begging for help and was totally distraught."

"I can imagine," Edith replied, shaking her head. "The Harkness family has always taken care of their own. The poor thing must be terrified."

"She is. David Wood and I are leaving for Nez Percé at eight o'clock. I'm sure Dave will be able to help her."

"Thanks," Edith replied as she sunk deeper into her chair. "I appreciate all you're doing for her. I'll be praying for her and her friends all day today. Be sure and call me as soon as you get back."

"I'll call as soon as I get back," Teresa replied. "Better yet, I'll have Dawn come see you herself." Teresa said good-bye to her friend and hung up the receiver. She was comforted by the knowledge that Edith Dutton would be praying.

The foothills of the Rocky Mountains were a somber backdrop as Teresa and Dave drove toward Nez Percé. Snow glistened from the distant peaks, but the drab, brown sagebrush and bare trees reflected the bleakness of the cold November morning.

Teresa rode in silence for many miles before she spoke. "Dave, what do you think will be the best way to handle the situation?"

"I've been pondering that myself ever since you called me." Dave hesitated. "Do you think Dawn has become a drug abuser since she went to college?"

"I'm afraid to even consider that possibility," Teresa sighed, "but last summer she was hanging out with some pretty rough kids. When she pledged Alpha Gamma Kappa sorority, her brother had a fit. He'd heard rumors about that particular sorority doing a lot of partying. Jay did everything he could to talk her out of pledging, but to no avail."

"That's not a very encouraging note," Dave said, shaking his head. "However, there's one thing in her favor. If she is using drugs, I don't think she's been using them very long. The less time she's been taking drugs, the better the chances of her getting off them altogether. I'm a firm believer in rehabilitation centers during the early stages of drug abuse."

Teresa's eyes drifted over the landscape. The sight of cattle grazing on the hillside usually lifted her spirit, but today the tranquility of the Montana scene conflicted with her internal struggles. *How can this be happening to a beautiful young woman from a fine Christian home?*

Teresa turned her attention back to her traveling companion. "But there is no rehabilitation center in Rocky Bluff," she protested weakly. "Dawn needs her family and friends now more than ever before in her life."

Dave nodded his head in agreement. "That's true," he replied, "but usually separation from family and friends for a short period of time gives drug users time to examine themselves and set new goals and objectives . . . without outside influence."

"That makes sense, but Dawn seems too young and innocent to be sent out of state," Teresa responded. "It's not like she doesn't have a family who loves and supports her."

"There's a center in Billings that I'm familiar with that might be helpful," Dave replied. "I've made arrangements for several of my clients to receive therapy at the Rimrock Rehabilitation Center. They all have come back to thank me for steering them in the right direction. Several of them had been addicted for a number of years and had a lot of other problems to overcome. If the center could help them, maybe it would be able to help Dawn as well."

For the remainder of the trip, Dave and Teresa discussed the services available at the Rimrock Rehabilitation Center. Both hoped that they would find Dawn a mere victim of being in the wrong place at the wrong time, but they feared the worst. Had she slipped from casual social drinking to heavy drinking to drug use? As they examined the change in her behavior since she had left for college, the case against her seemed overwhelming. Her grades had dropped. She no longer cared about her personal appearance. She avoided the people and places that had once been important in her life. The few times she had returned to Rocky Bluff, her eyes were distant and glazed. Her mother had commented on her increased moodiness.

When they arrived in Nez Percé, they went directly to the Chief Joseph County Jail. The deputy led them to the visitors' room, and shivers crept down Teresa's spine when the barred door of the jail slammed behind them.

Teresa paced nervously around the room

until Dawn entered. She was thinner than Teresa had remembered her, and her eyes were red and swollen from crying. She rushed into Teresa's arms, sobbing.

"I'm sorry. . . . I'm such a fool. . . . I've ruined my entire life. . . . I've disgraced the Harkness name."

Teresa held her until her crying subsided. Dave seated Dawn at the small conference table and nodded to Teresa. "Now tell us exactly what happened," the older woman insisted gently but firmly. "We'll do our best to help, but we have to know every detail that happened."

Dawn fidgeted nervously as the words tumbled from her mouth. "One of the fraternity guys invited our sorority to a party at his parents' ranch while they were away." She twisted a lock of her hair around her index finger. "I don't know how the sheriff's department heard about the party, but they turned up around midnight. Nearly everyone was drinking beer, but the police were looking only for drugs. They arrested six of us for using cocaine."

Dave looked at Dawn gravely. "Were you using cocaine?"

Dawn's eyes fell to the floor. Her face flushed. "Yes," she whispered.

"How long have you been using drugs?"

Dave persisted.

Dawn did not lift her eyes as she muttered, "I started a year and a half ago when I first went to college."

"What kinds of drugs have you used?"

Dawn choked back her sobs as she stared blankly at the tiled floor. "First it was just drinking, then I tried marijuana. I started sniffing coke about three months ago. I'm not addicted to it or anything like that. It just helps relieve the stress of my classes. Whenever I'm faced with a big test, a little cocaine helps me get through it."

Dave shook his head. "You are faced with a very serious charge," he said softly. "You are charged with possession and use of a controlled substance. The judge may not be very lenient. I suggest you agree to enroll in the Rimrock Rehabilitation Center in Billings. They have an excellent success rate, and the judge will be more inclined to give you a break as a first offender."

"But I'm not addicted," Dawn persisted. "I just wanted to have some fun and relieve my stress."

"Judges don't accept that logic," Dave replied sternly. "They could fine you and send you to jail. If I were the one making the choice, I'd choose rehabilitation over jail."

Dawn's jaw dropped, and her face turned ashen. "You mean it's that serious?"

Dave nodded his head. "It's that serious."

Tears again filled Dawn's eyes. "Do you think I'll have to stay here until my parents get home?"

"I'll talk to the judge if you'll promise to go to the rehab center as soon as there is an opening. This might be your only way to prevent having a criminal record," Dave explained. "If he agrees, I'll ask that you be released to Teresa's custody until you enter rehab."

Dawn thought a moment, then turned to Teresa. "Are you sure you want to do this?"

Teresa took Dawn's hand and looked into the frightened young woman's eyes. "Of course I do. If we all work together, you'll be back in college in no time."

The next few hours were hectic for all three of them. The court released Dawn to Teresa's custody and arranged for Dawn to enter the Rimrock Rehabilitation Center in three days. Teresa signed the necessary papers, and Dawn agreed to avoid all drugs and alcohol.

Late that afternoon, Dave, Teresa, and Dawn drove to Dawn's sorority house and packed her belongings. The next stop was the registrar's office, where Dawn withdrew from college but retained the right to reenroll at a later time.

By five o'clock the three were on their way to Rocky Bluff. After a day of tension and frustration, the sunset's red glow behind the mountains relaxed the trio. Dawn was soon asleep in the backseat. Her blond hair framed her petite face, giving her an air of innocence that belied her recent experiences. She did not awaken until the lights of Rocky Bluff shone through the windows of David Wood's car.

"Can we go see Grandma as soon as we unload the car?" Dawn asked shyly. "I know I've been a lot of trouble to everyone today, but it would mean so much if I could see her. When I was a little girl, I used to crawl up in her lap, and she always seemed to make everything right again."

Teresa turned around in her seat. "Of course," she agreed. "I promised her I'd either call or bring you over just as soon as we got back to town."

Dave parked his car in Teresa's driveway, and the three hurriedly carried suitcases and boxes into Teresa's spare bedroom. As Dave set the last box in the corner, Dawn extended her hand. "Thanks for all your help. I don't know what I'd have done without you," she murmured, her face red. "Rehab will be a lot better than going to jail. But I still don't think I'm an addict."

Dave smiled at her and placed his hand on her shoulder. "I'm looking forward to talking with you next month after you have been through treatment. You'll see drug use in an entirely different light then," he said. "Good luck. I'll be praying for you."

While Dave backed his car down the driveway, Teresa and Dawn hurried to the garage. They were silent as they drove the familiar streets to Edith Dutton's home. Dawn's mind drifted back to the day when her grandmother had moved here from the spacious, two-story family home. She had turned the large house over to her son and grandchildren, and Dawn remembered the joy of unpacking the treasures she had collected in the first seven years of her life in her upstairs bedroom. She pictured her grandmother's wedding with Roy Dutton and the fun she had had with them. A lump built in her throat as she thought about Roy's stroke and the year he had spent in the nursing home before he passed away. Roy had been a welcomed replacement for the grandfather who had died before she was born.

Dawn scarcely waited for Teresa to stop

her car in front of the Dutton home before she sprang from the front seat and bounded up the sidewalk. Before she could reach the doorbell, Edith flung open the door and wrapped her frail arms around her granddaughter. "Grandma, Grandma. I'm sorry," Dawn gasped. "I've let everyone down. I've never had such a terrible experience in my life."

Edith motioned for Teresa to close the door behind her, then led the trembling young woman to the sofa. "Dawn, tell me everything that happened," she insisted gently. "There's nothing so bad that God and the Harkness family can't handle together."

For the next two hours, Dawn poured out the details of her guilt and fears. Teresa was amazed at the loving acceptance Edith showed her wayward granddaughter. So often when she had worked with people in trouble, their families would turn their backs on the struggling person until they had regained some level of acceptability. But Edith's love for her granddaughter never wavered.

Edith gently tried to move Dawn from the denial of her addiction to admitting that drugs had taken control of her life, but the beautiful young coed was still not ready to accept the impact that drugs were having on her life.

After she had poured out her heart to her grandmother, Dawn noticed the dark circles gathering under the old woman's eyes. "Grandma, I didn't mean to keep you up so late. I better let you get some rest. I'll come and see you before I leave for Billings." Dawn stood to leave.

"Get a good night's rest," Edith replied as she hugged her granddaughter. "I'll be praying for you."

"Thanks, Grandma." Dawn returned the hug. "There's one other thing. If Mom or Dad call, would you tell them what happened and let them know how sorry I am to disgrace the Harkness name? Don't let them cut their vacation short on my account. They've saved for this trip for years. They deserve every moment of relaxation they can get."

"I'll do the best I can," Edith assured her, "but knowing your parents, they'll probably be on the next plane back to Rocky Bluff."

Dawn slept most of the next day. The security of being home in Rocky Bluff relaxed her tension-filled body. When she awoke, she began pondering drug rehabilitation and bombarded Teresa with questions.

Teresa went through her files until she found several brochures, pamphlets, and a book on the subject. Dawn spent the rest of the evening poring over them. She searched for any clue as to what the future might hold for her.

The next morning, Dawn arose early, showered, and was waiting in the living room when Teresa stumbled to the kitchen with her eyes only partially opened.

"Good morning," Dawn greeted as she looked up from the morning paper.

"You're up early for a Sunday morning," Teresa replied. "You look nice today."

"I want to go to church with you," Dawn replied. "I haven't gone since I went to college, and I think I better get back in the habit. Maybe if I hadn't ignored what my parents taught me about walking daily with God, I wouldn't be in this mess."

Teresa smiled and nodded with agreement. "Your family did give you a firm foundation, and Pastor Rhodes has always been available to teach and console those who have needed him."

"He's the only minister I've ever known," Dawn replied. "Every time there was a high point in my life he was always there. Now he's here during the lowest point in my life.

I'd like to talk with him before I leave for Billings."

Dawn fixed breakfast, while Teresa dressed. After they had eaten, they drove to Edith's house to give her a ride to church. Since Bob and Nancy were gone, Edith was left without transportation.

The church service that Sunday took on a special meaning for Dawn. She squeezed her grandmother's hand as she recited the Lord's Prayer. *"Forgive us our trespasses as we forgive those who trespass against us."* The hymns, the sermon, and the prayers seemed to have been tailored just for her. After the closing hymn, instead of walking to the back to greet the people, Pastor Rhodes motioned for the congregation to be seated. Everyone exchanged puzzled glances as they quickly obeyed.

"I have some sad but exciting news for you," Pastor Rhodes began. "The first of January, I will be leaving Rocky Bluff to accept the pastorate in Sheridan, Wyoming. I am leaving this congregation with deep regret. We have shared many years of joys and sorrows and have grown together as a family of God. I will miss you greatly, but there comes a time for change. I now feel it is time for me to move on and turn this congregation over to a younger minister. I trust you will receive your new pastor with the same love and acceptance you have shown to me."

Dawn didn't hear any more of Pastor Rhodes's farewell speech. Just when she needed him the most, he would be leaving them. No one would ever be able to fill his place in her life. By the time Dawn completed drug treatment, a new minister would be in the pulpit, and church would never be the same again.

# Chapter 2

Dawn Harkness gazed out the window of the Rimrock Rehabilitation Center. Tears filled her eyes as she watched her grandmother and Teresa Lennon leave the parking lot. *I shouldn't be here,* she mused as Teresa's car turned the corner and went out of sight. *I should be back in the sorority house. I'm not a drug addict like the others here. What will my parents think when they get back from the Caribbean? I have humiliated the Harkness name. Grandma was so gracious about helping me, but I could see the pain underneath her smile. She didn't deserve to see me here.*

"It's hard to say good-bye, isn't it?" a voice behind her said as a gentle hand was placed on her shoulder.

Dawn turned to face a tall brunette dressed in a comfortable sweater and jeans. "I shouldn't be here," Dawn protested. "I'm not an addict. I only used drugs at a few parties to relieve the stress of college life, and now I'm an embarrassment to my entire family."

"That's the way I felt when I first came," the other young woman replied. "It looks like we're going to be roommates for several weeks so it's time we became acquainted. Let's go down to the rec room, and I'll buy you a soft drink."

"Thanks," Dawn replied. "I guess I'll have to make the best of a bad situation."

The two young women strolled down the wide corridor to the recreation center. "It's not so bad here once you get used to it," the tall young woman said. "My name's Lori Hauser. I'm from Missoula. What's your name?"

"Dawn . . . Dawn Harkness. I'm from Rocky Bluff, but I went to college at Montana A&M. Being here is ruining one entire semester." Dawn selected her favorite soft drink from the vending machine. She shrugged her shoulders as a can slammed into the bin at the bottom of the machine. "I suppose it doesn't matter. . . . My grades were falling anyway."

Lori led the way to a table for two in the corner. "You sound just like I did when I came here three weeks ago," she chuckled.

"The counselors and other residents helped me understand what casual use of drugs was doing to my body and my life. I've had to reexamine my life and attitudes from the very beginning. It was touch and go for awhile. I didn't have a very pretty picture of myself, but I figure it will be worth it in the end. My family's coming next week for family week, and I can hardly wait."

Dawn wrinkled her forehead. "What's family week?"

"After a resident is here about three weeks, they encourage the entire family to come and stay for a week. Drug addiction is not just an individual's problem. It affects the entire family."

"But I wasn't using drugs when I was living at home. My using drugs had nothing to do with my family. It was my own choice. They'll be horrified when they get back and find out where I am." Dawn gazed out the window as a light snow began to fall on the barren tree limbs. "If I hadn't gotten arrested at a party, they would never have known I was using drugs."

Lori looked at her new friend with understanding. "Hiding your drug use from your family is one of the first signs of addiction," she said softly. "Denial is one of the defenses we use to escape accepting the reality of drug addiction. It's the major stumbling block to a cure."

Dawn continued gazing out the window. *Maybe I am an addict. Some people at school have taken drugs a lot longer than I have, and they're still in control of their own lives. But somehow I seemed to lose control right away.* She turned her attention back to her new friend. "Lori, perhaps I was headed toward addiction, but it's not a big deal yet. I could quit any time I wanted. I've only used cocaine at parties. If the cops hadn't gotten word of my last party, no one would have known the difference."

Lori shook her head. "Minimizing is another defense against accepting reality." She laughed and shook her head. "I'm sorry. Three weeks ago I was saying the exact things you are. And here I am now, quoting the counselors word for word. But it's true. Believe me, I know. I was one of those people who say their drug problem's no big deal, even when I had nearly destroyed my life. Admit it. Drugs were destroying your life too, otherwise you wouldn't be here."

Anger danced in Dawn's eyes. "Your experiences were different than mine," she said coldly. "I don't have to sit here and be insulted." She rushed from the rec room in tears.

Others relaxing in the room looked up from the TV corner. "What's wrong with her?" one of them asked.

"She's new. She's having trouble accepting her problems. Give her a couple of days, and she'll be fine," Lori explained as she joined the group watching television. "She doesn't understand that we've all been through the same thing."

Dawn ran to her room and flopped across her bed. Pain vibrated through her, spreading out from her heart, until she curled into a ball and rocked herself back and forth. *If only I had some cocaine. The stress I felt at college is nothing compared to this. Why did Lori assume I'm in a state of denial or that I'm minimizing my problem? She seemed nice until she brought up all the defense mechanisms she thinks I'm using. She sounded so sure of herself, like she knew all the answers just because she's been here three weeks. Three weeks couldn't possibly make that much difference. I'll stay here because I don't want to go to jail, but I won't change my mind. They're not going to brainwash me into believing I'm an addict.*

Shadows fell across the room as the sun

set behind the distant Beartooth Mountains. As Dawn's sobs subsided, she drifted into a deep sleep. She did not hear Lori slip quietly into the room, prepare for bed, and crawl beneath the blankets in the bed across the room.

The room remained quiet until six-thirty the next morning when a loud ringing from down the hall caused Dawn to bolt upright in bed. "What's that?"

"Just our morning wake-up," Lori laughed. "They don't want us to sleep a minute past six-thirty. Then they give us only forty-five minutes to shower, dress, make our beds, and get to breakfast. It takes me that long just to get my makeup on."

Dawn threw back the covers, slipped her feet into her slippers, and trudged to the bathroom. Her movements were robotlike, the emotions of the last few days repressed. Her consciousness could not deal with more pain.

Nancy and Bob Harkness and their son and daughter-in-law, Jay and Angie, stepped off the airplane in Great Falls, Montana, and mingled with the crowd who hurried toward the baggage claim. "I'll go get the car," Jay volunteered. "I hope I won't have any trouble starting it. Leaving it parked for weeks in this cold weather isn't too good on the engine."

"We'll get your luggage and meet you in the loading zone," Bob replied.

A cold blast of winter wind hit Jay in the face as he stepped outside the airport building. He wrapped his light sweater tighter around himself as he jogged across the parking lot. *I'm glad we left our winter coats in the car.* He fumbled with the key, opened the front door, and reached over the seat for his coat. He breathed a sigh of relief as he pulled the fleece-lined suede coat over his shoulders. After three weak shudders, the engine started; he idled it for a few minutes, then drove to the loading zone. Spotting his family waiting behind the entrance windows, he put the engine in neutral, grabbed their coats, and rushed inside.

Within minutes the luggage was loaded into the trunk and the Harkness family was on their way home to Rocky Bluff. Nancy leaned her head back against the seat. "That was the most fantastic vacation we've ever had. It's too bad Dawn wasn't able to go with us."

"If I remember right, we offered to postpone the trip until her semester break, but she said she wasn't interested in going on any yuppie vacation trip," Jay reminded her.

"I know," his mother sighed. "It's just a phase she's going through. It won't be long before she discovers the value of being with her family." Nancy admired her tall, dark-haired son behind the wheel of the car. *God has been so good to our family,* she mused. *Our family has shared a lot of joys and pain, and we've always come out stronger and more unified.* "I remember how anxious you were to get out of Rocky Bluff when you graduated from high school. You joined the Air Force and requested an assignment in Guam, as far away from Montana as you could get," she chided.

"I'm glad he did," Angie giggled. "Otherwise I'd never have met Jay and found out how beautiful Montana is."

Jay nodded his head and smiled. "Just think, Mom, you'll be the only one in Rocky Bluff who'll have half-Guamanian grandchildren," he teased.

Bob, who had appeared to be dozing, instantly straightened his back. "Son, are you trying to tell us something?"

"We're not sure yet," Jay replied, "but Angie went to the drugstore while we were in St. Croix and bought a home pregnancy test, and she passed with flying colors!

Please don't tell anyone until she's had time to go to the doctor to have it confirmed. We don't want to get our hopes up, then be disappointed."

Nancy nearly burst with excitement. "I hope you make an appointment first thing in the morning. This is news to be shouted from the housetops of Rocky Bluff."

"I plan to," Angie assured them as she squeezed her husband's hand.

For the rest of the trip, Jay rotated gospel tapes in the car stereo, while his family dozed or idly watched the landscape fly by. The end of a perfect vacation had climaxed with the possibility of another generation of Harknesses.

The next morning, Nancy sat relaxing in her robe over her morning cup of coffee. Bob had left early for the hardware store, and a pile of laundry was beckoning her. Suddenly, her calm was interrupted by the loud ringing of the telephone. She picked up the phone.

"Hello?"

"Hello, Nancy," answered Teresa's voice. "It's good to have you home."

"Hi, Teresa. I'm glad you called. I'm anxious to hear everything that happened in Rocky Bluff while we were gone. There was something wrong with the connection the last time we tried to call Bob's mother, so I'm way behind on the news."

Teresa gulped. The news she had for her dearest friend was not going to be easy to tell. "We have a lot to talk about. How about if I come over in about a half hour?"

"Spending time with my best friend will be a lot more fun than facing a pile of laundry."

After she'd hung up the phone, Nancy hurried to the bedroom and pulled on a pair of blue sweats, then tied her hair back with a bow. When the doorbell rang, she flung the door open and embraced her friend.

"I didn't hurry you, did I?" Teresa asked, trying to hide the tension in her voice. "I figured after a vacation to the Caribbean you'd be sleeping late for a week."

"Oh, no. I was up early. Bob was anxious to get to the store. The Christmas merchandise is beginning to arrive, and he wanted to get everything displayed as soon as possible."

Nancy poured two cups of coffee, while Teresa brought her up to date on the minor happenings of Rocky Bluff. After Nancy was seated at the table, Teresa became serious. "Nancy, Dawn had a major problem while you were gone, and she needs you now more than ever before in her life."

A deep furrow creased Nancy's forehead. "What happened?"

"She was at a party at a ranch outside of Nez Percé, and the sheriff's department arrived and arrested six of them for using illegal drugs. She called me from jail in the middle of the night. She didn't know what to do, and they wouldn't release her unless her parents were there, and she didn't know how to get ahold of you. She was hysterical."

Nancy's face blanched. "What happened? Where is she now?"

"Dave Wood went to Nez Percé with me. He was able to convince the judge to release her into our custody if she would consent to drug treatment at the Rimrock Rehabilitation Center in Billings. Dawn wasn't very pleased with the idea, but she figured it was better than sitting in jail and having a criminal record."

Nancy stared at the floor in silence. Never before had anyone in her family been on the wrong side of the law. She choked back a sob. "Do you think she was actually using drugs?"

"I'm afraid so," Teresa replied. "She admitted that she started using cocaine last summer. Edith rode with me when I drove her to Billings a week ago Sunday. Dawn was certain she had humiliated the Harkness name, but her grandmother did her best to convince her that regardless of what happened, her family would always love her."

"When can I talk to her? She can't go through this alone," Nancy objected.

"I understand she has a pretty heavy schedule of lectures, individual and group therapy, and assignments. I'll give you the name and number of the director of the center, and she'll be able to put you in contact with Dawn."

The muscles in Nancy's neck tightened. "Bob and I will need to go to Billings to see her right away."

"Residents aren't allowed to have guests until family week, which is usually the third week of the treatment. During that week, the families stay at the center and go through therapy with the resident. There's a much greater success rate if the entire family participates."

Nancy rose. Her hand trembled. "I better call Bob and have him come home so you can explain this to him as well. I'll also give Jay a call. I don't think he had to be to work until noon today. It's time for a family meeting, and we need your expertise to help us through this. I don't know what we'd do without friends like you."

Two weeks later, Dawn, Jay, Angie, Nancy, and Bob Harkness gathered in the family therapy room in the Rimrock Rehabilitation Center. Dawn sat tensely as she surveyed the faces of her family. Even though each affirmed their love, Dawn was unconvinced. She felt she had committed an unforgivable sin in defaming the family name.

"Dawn, can you tell us when you began to feel estranged from your family?" the therapist asked.

Dawn stared at the floor. She sat in silence for several long minutes. "Everything changed when I was in junior high school," she murmured. "Everyone was so wrapped up in Jay's basketball and football that no one seemed to care if I was around or not. The entire town seemed to worship basketball and its stars. I felt that if a person wasn't good in sports they weren't worth having around."

"Honey, that's not true. We've always loved you both equally," Nancy protested. "You excelled in music, while Jay excelled in sports."

"Not very many people came to my music concerts," Dawn retorted. "Those who did were there only because their kid was performing. They sat there bored to death during the rest of the performance. But those same people talked about ball games for weeks afterward."

"That may be an accurate observation," Bob noted, "but that doesn't negate your accomplishments."

Dawn continued to pour out real and imagined situations that had upset her, and the family explained their perception of the same events. Dawn told how she felt pushed aside when Angie had come to Rocky Bluff. With that, Angie broke into tears.

"I didn't mean to hurt you," Angie sobbed. "I liked you, and I tried so hard to get you to like me. I wanted so badly to be accepted by you and your friends, but you always excluded me."

With that, Dawn broke down crying as well. "I wanted to be with you, but my friends didn't want a foreigner marrying the handsomest guy in town. They wanted him for themselves." When her sobs subsided, Dawn got up and wrapped her arms around her sister-in-law. "I'm sorry I hurt you. I'm proud to have you married to my brother. I knew you were so much better and kinder than the girls I was hanging around with, but I wanted to feel accepted by that crowd.

Look at what it got me. I'd hate to have any of them as a member of the family."

Little by little as the week progressed, the wall Dawn had built around herself crumbled. Everyone accepted responsibility for their role in the situation. They confessed their sins to each other and to God and begged each other's forgiveness. They prayed together in total unity. Never before had the therapist observed the true inner healing that only God can provide.

Before the week was over, the therapist began exploring Dawn's future with the Harkness family.

"I'd like to go back to college next fall," Dawn explained, "but I don't feel strong enough to be separated from my family right now. I'm so emotionally drained and vulnerable. Can I come home and work in the store?"

"Of course you can," Bob replied as he squeezed his daughter's hand. "In fact, it would be a big help to us. Our bookkeeper wants to take some time off to stay home with her family, and I didn't know how I was going to replace her."

"If you returned to Rocky Bluff, you would still need to have some form of aftercare," the therapist reminded Dawn. "As far as I know, Rocky Bluff does not have any facilities for follow-up care."

"Psychological help is very limited in rural Montana," Bob reminded the therapist, "but Teresa Lennon has a master's degree in psychiatric social work. She has helped hundreds of young women at the Spouse Abuse Shelter."

The entire Harkness family nodded their heads simultaneously. Angie was the first to speak. "When I was going through a difficult time in my life, Teresa was the one who helped me get my life back together. It meant so much to have a trained therapist who understood my Christian faith."

The therapist nodded. "Yes," she said thoughtfully, "after seeing your family in action this week, I think I can understand that. Dawn, let me call Teresa Lennon and see if we can work out a plan for your aftercare."

When their last family therapy session was over, the therapist thanked each one of them for participating. "I've never seen this kind of love and support from a family and community for any of our residents before," she admitted. "I'll make arrangements for Dawn to return to Rocky Bluff within the next ten days. Good luck to all of you. It was a pleasure to work with such a concerned, compassionate family."

The family said good-bye to Dawn and prepared for their trip home. Farewells were hard to say, but each knew they were preparing for a new beginning with Dawn back in her rightful place in the family.

# CHAPTER 3

Teresa Lennon leaned back in her chair in the minister's study of the Rocky Bluff Community Church. "Pastor Rhodes, you don't know how much I hate to see you leave," she admitted sadly. "Now that the court has assigned Dawn Harkness's case to me, I need all the support I can get."

"Teresa, I have confidence in your expertise," Pastor Rhodes replied. "You've been in the counseling business for a long while and have handled life-threatening situations. I'm certain you'll be able to handle Dawn's situation as well." The pastor's compassionate, gray eyes surveyed the woman across his desk. Leaving Rocky Bluff after nearly twenty years of ministry was going to hurt. He had seen an entire generation of children grow up, and he had watched people like Teresa climb from the beginning of their career to the peak of their productivity.

"My experience is all with spousal abuse,

not drug abuse," Teresa answered. "Up until now, we've had few cases of drug abuse in Rocky Bluff. The situation is even more difficult because I've been a family friend of the Harknesses ever since I moved here."

"Your friendship with the family could be more of an asset than a detriment," Pastor Rhodes said.

Teresa nodded. "I know. It's just . . ." She sighed. "Dawn seems to have a deep sense of guilt. She's going through an intense spiritual struggle. I'm not sure my counseling skills will be enough. I think she's going to need pastoral counseling as well. She's very upset that you're leaving, especially now in the midst of this crisis."

"Remember, all things work together for good in God's kingdom." Pastor Rhodes stroked his chin. "Besides, God's grace does not depend on any one person. Fortunately, the new minister will be here this weekend. I understand he had undergraduate training in alcohol- and drug-abuse counseling."

"He could be a great help." But Teresa was not really convinced. "What's his name?"

"Bryan Olson. He's in his late forties, never married, and totally committed to his profession."

A wry smile spread across Teresa's face.

"It's going to be different for our church not to have a pastor's wife. We've come to depend too much on Mrs. Rhodes. She's had to do tasks over and above the call of duty."

"Rest assured," Pastor Rhodes replied, "she enjoyed every minute of it. This congregation has truly become our family."

"At least Rev. Olson is beyond the age of everyone trying to play matchmaker for him," Teresa chuckled. "Nothing is more repulsive than overanxious mothers trying to marry their daughters off to the local minister."

Pastor Rhodes's laughter mingled with Teresa's. "I've known of a situation where the competition among the mothers nearly tore a church apart. The funny part about that competition was that not one of the daughters was the least bit interested in the young minister."

"The life of a minister's wife has got to be the most difficult one in a community," Teresa said. "She would always have someone criticizing her, regardless of what she does. Her time would never be her own. That's one role I've never wanted."

"Yes, there is a downside to parsonage life." Pastor Rhodes nodded his head. "However, Emily would not have had it any other way. She loves helping people. The hardest part was raising our family in the spotlight. After the children were grown, she found things easier. That's when she truly began to thrive in her role as a pastor's wife."

"Both of your children turned out well in spite of the public scrutiny," Teresa protested. "That speaks well of their home life."

The older minister's eyes grew distant. "We tried our best to maintain a certain amount of family privacy while they were growing up. Few people realized the personal struggles we were going through behind closed doors. It wasn't easy . . . but God was faithful."

Teresa watched the gentleness that shone in the pastor's face. She had not realized how fond of him she had become until she faced the reality of his moving. "Hopefully, the new minister will be able to relate to Dawn. I'm not trained to deal with all her problems," she sighed. "When the court assigned her to me, they didn't recognize the difference between spiritual, emotional, and drug-related problems." She glanced at her watch, and her forehead wrinkled. "Oh no. I didn't realize it was getting so late. I need to be at the shelter by three."

Teresa bid the minister farewell, then hurried to her car. As she drove, she wondered if the new minister would be able to help Dawn. *In all my years working with spouse abuse cases, I've never known a confirmed bachelor who could understand a woman's emotional pain well enough to help her. Unmarried men always seem to have textbook answers to personal problems.*

After her meeting, she drove home, looking forward to a relaxing evening at home. She had just changed into comfortable clothes when the telephone rang.

"Hello?"

"Hello, Teresa," said Nancy's voice. "I was wondering if you'd like to come along on Friday when we bring Dawn home."

Teresa glanced at her daily planner. "I'd love to," she replied. "It's about the only day I have free this week. Saturday I'm going to be decorating the fellowship hall for the pastor's farewell dinner."

The two continued to chat about Dawn's homecoming and the community dinner for their pastor. Both avoided the underlying question nagging them. *How will Dawn readjust back into the community after having been through rehabilitation? Will she remain strong enough to resist temptation from her peers?*

■ ■ ■ ■

On Saturday evening more than two hundred people crowded into the fellowship hall of the Rocky Bluff Community Church. While everyone else gorged themselves with the potluck dinner, Dawn pushed her food back and forth with her fork, a lump in her throat. "Teresa, how am I going to get along without Pastor Rhodes? I need a minister now more than ever."

"The new minister will be at church tomorrow," Teresa whispered. "I'm sure you'll like him. He's a bachelor who comes to us highly recommended."

"If he's never been married, how can he possibly understand what a woman goes through, especially one who's had as many problems as I've had?" Dawn protested.

"Dawn, give him a chance," Teresa persisted. "He may be the answer to our prayers. They say he had a tremendous ministry to alcohol and drug addicts in Boise."

Dawn shook her head. "He might have been able to work with the men, but I doubt if he was able to help even one woman. If a man gets into his late forties and has never been married, something must be wrong

51

with him."

Teresa frowned as she felt the eyes of others at their table waiting for her response. "That's not always true," she replied softly. "Remember all the years our fire chief, Andy Hatfield, was a bachelor before he married Rebecca. He was so committed to his job that he never developed a personal life until Rebecca taught him how to slow down and enjoy life."

Dawn shrugged her shoulders and sneered. "But Andy's different. Most normal men are married before they're thirty."

With those words Teresa flushed, and everyone at their table looked away in embarrassment. The Dawn they had once known had never spoken in such a hard, cold voice. What had happened to the lovely Harkness daughter who had been the pride and joy of the family?

The next morning, Dawn was sitting with her parents in the back of the church when Teresa and Edith Dutton joined them. "Good morning, Dawn," her grandmother whispered as she slid in beside her granddaughter. "You're looking good today."

Just then a hush spread throughout the congregation as Pastor Rhodes entered the sanctuary followed by a handsome, middle-aged man with graying temples. After the usual hymns, Scripture readings, and prayers, Pastor Rhodes introduced the new pastor to the congregation. Then Pastor Rhodes sat down, and Pastor Olson began his sermon on love and forgiveness.

*Maybe he won't be so bad after all,* Teresa mused. *I hope he'll be able to relate to Dawn.*

Every evening after work, Dawn met with Teresa. Teresa became more and more concerned about her, for during each session she appeared more depressed than the day before. Dawn seemed to be holding something back. Finally, Friday afternoon Dawn entered Teresa's home crying.

Teresa ran to her side and wrapped her arms around the young woman. "Dawn, what's wrong?"

"I've disgraced my family," she sobbed.

"What happened? When you left Billings, you felt you had the most loving, accepting family possible and that all was forgiven."

"I did then, but I was wrong," Dawn replied. "No one else in town understands what happened. They're all talking about the Harkness drug addict. They're wondering what other secrets our family is hiding behind closed doors."

Teresa led the shaking woman to the sofa.

"Whatever gave you such an idea?"

"I heard a couple of old ladies talking about me in the restaurant today." Dawn's voice trembled. "You know how tall the dividers between the booths are at the Main Street Grill. They didn't see me sitting there, so they said the cruelest things."

"But who cares what they said?" Teresa questioned. "You know the truth, and what happened is none of their business."

"I know that." Dawn wiped her tears with the back of her hand. "But they said they were going to quit buying at Harkness Hardware because as long as I was working there I could be selling drugs and using the store as a cover."

Teresa's mouth tightened. "That's the most ridiculous thing I've ever heard."

"Don't you see," Dawn shouted, "it's not just me. I've hurt and humiliated the entire family. I wish I were dead."

"Dawn, please don't talk that way. You're a forgiven sinner whom Christ died for. God knows the truth; that's all that counts."

"No," Dawn sobbed. "I've hurt and destroyed the very people I love the most. I've committed the unpardonable sin."

"I don't fully understand what the unpardonable sin is, but the Bible says it is blasphemy against the Holy Spirit. I've never heard you do that," Teresa replied. "You're just extremely hurt by what you heard today."

"No. I've committed the unpardonable sin. Everyone would be better off if I were dead."

Teresa's mind raced. She knew she was being faced with the threat of suicide, but she felt helpless to assist Dawn with her spiritual struggle. How could she, when she didn't even know what the unpardonable sin was herself? Teresa knew she needed expert guidance immediately. "Dawn, I can't answer some of your questions about sin. Would you permit me to call our new pastor? He's been trained to handle such questions."

"But I'd rather talk to Pastor Rhodes," Dawn protested.

"I know," Teresa sighed. "I would too, but we have to accept the fact that he's not here any longer. Wait here while I call Pastor Olson."

Teresa hurriedly pushed the buttons on her phone's keypad. As she listened to the phone ring, she breathed a silent prayer for help.

"Hello, Pastor Olson speaking," a voice finally answered.

"Pastor Olson, this is Teresa Lennon. I

met you Sunday in church. I'm the director of the Spouse Abuse Shelter. I have a young woman in my home who is a member of our church. She is going through a very difficult time and is extremely despondent. She is sure she has committed the unpardonable sin. Would you possibly be able to come over and meet with us? I feel we're in a crisis situation right now."

The pleading in Teresa's voice sent a shiver down the pastor's spine. He understood the message she was conveying, for he had worked with potential suicide cases before. This was his first major challenge in Rocky Bluff, and he knew the respect of his congregation might depend on how he handled this crisis.

"Teresa, where are you located?"

Teresa told him.

"I'll be right there," Pastor Olson promised.

Dawn had stretched out on the sofa, her face buried in the cushions. Teresa hung up the phone, then balanced herself on the corner of the sofa and put her hand on Dawn's trembling shoulder. "Dawn, please turn over and talk with me. You can't hide from your problems this way."

Dawn continued sobbing, while Teresa gently rubbed her back. Dawn seemed oblivious to her counselor's presence; all Teresa could do was wait and pray that the new minister would be able to relieve Dawn's distress.

When the doorbell rang, Teresa ran to greet Pastor Bryan Olson. In a soft voice, she quickly explained Dawn's drug abuse problem and her experience at the Rimrock Rehabilitation Center. Pastor Olson nodded and entered Teresa's living room. He pulled his chair close to the sofa where the sobbing young woman lay.

Instead of talking directly to Dawn, he lifted his eyes toward heaven. "Heavenly Father," he prayed, "please shower Your love and mercy down on Dawn. Ease her broken heart and take away her pain. Let her feel Your presence. Give her the assurance of her salvation through the death and resurrection of Jesus Christ."

With each passing word, Dawn's sobs became softer and further apart. When Pastor Olson finished praying, Dawn rolled over and sat up, tucking her feet under her. "Thank you," she murmured.

"How are you doing, Dawn?" he asked kindly.

She looked down at her hands. "I'm a disgrace to God, my family, and the entire community. I don't deserve to live."

"None of us deserves to live," Pastor Olson replied.

A look of shock spread across Dawn's face. "Teresa, my family, and especially my grandmother deserve the very best. They're such good people. I love all of them so much. They're always helping others without thinking about themselves."

"Even the best of people are still sinful in God's eyes," Pastor Olson reminded her. "But because of Christ's death we are covered with a robe of righteousness. When you cling to Christ, you become the same in God's eyes as any saint."

Dawn sat motionless for several minutes. The words of the gospel slowly cut through her bruised emotions. "That's what Grandma always told me," she finally whispered. "I never fully understood what she was telling me until now."

For the next two hours, Dawn poured out her frustrations, while Pastor Olson shared Christ's love and understanding with her. Teresa watched with amazement. *To think I thought that a confirmed bachelor would never understand the emotions and pain of a woman,* she scolded herself. *He seems to have a direct pipeline to heaven and knows the exact words to say to help her. All my years of psychological training never prepared me for this moment.*

Gradually, Dawn began to relax, and finally, she was able to lift her head and look directly at the pastor.

"Dawn, you look awfully tired." Pastor Olson watched the way the young woman sat wilted on the sofa with the back of her head against the cushion.

"I am," she admitted. "The only other time I've ever cried like this was my first night at the rehabilitation center."

"Tears can be God's healing medicine," Pastor Olson replied softly. "Why don't we have Teresa call your mother to give you a ride home? I suggest you stay home tomorrow and rest. I'll check with you later in the day."

Dawn nodded, and Teresa hurried to the phone. She dialed the familiar number, then explained the situation.

When Nancy arrived, she hugged her daughter, who immediately begged for forgiveness. After assuring her daughter that she was forgiven and she was still loved dearly, Nancy turned to the others. "I want to thank you for helping us. I don't know what we'd do without you. I feel so helpless. It seems like I ought to be able to help my own daughter better."

"It's often the hardest to help those we love the most." Pastor Olson placed his hand on Nancy's shoulder and walked them to the door.

Teresa hugged Dawn. "Be sure to call me whenever you're feeling alone and discouraged. That's what I'm here for."

Dawn nodded, and Teresa then turned to Nancy. "You've got a lovely daughter. I'm glad I'm the one allowed to share her difficult moments. With God's help she's going to have a beautiful future." Nancy smiled as she accepted Teresa's words of comfort.

As soon as the door closed behind the Harknesses, Teresa breathed a heavy sigh of relief and turned to the minister. She noticed that he too looked emotionally drained. "Pastor Olson, would you like a cup of coffee before you go?"

The minister collapsed onto the sofa. "I'd appreciate that," he replied with a smile, "but please call me Bryan. I think we're going to be working together a great deal in the next few months."

# Chapter 4

"Nancy, do you think we have enough lights on the tree?" Teresa stepped back to admire the twelve-foot-high Christmas tree that adorned the front corner of the church sanctuary. "It looks kind of skimpy toward the top."

Nancy's eyes drifted toward the angel on the top of the tree. The white lights ended nearly two feet from the angel's skirts, and Nancy couldn't mask her amusement. "It does look pretty bad, doesn't it?" she giggled. "I'll run to the hardware store and get more lights, while you finish putting the boughs on the windowsills."

"Greenery is one thing we have plenty of," Teresa noted as she headed toward a huge box of boughs in the corner. "The youth group had a good time going to the woods. It's a wonder none of the kids were hurt with all the chopping they must have been doing."

"Don't worry, I was with them," a voice said from behind them.

Teresa and Nancy wheeled around and found their pastor walking down the aisle toward them.

Bryan chuckled at their startled faces. "I didn't mean to sneak up on you. Incidentally, I worked my way through undergraduate school by fighting forest fires in Idaho, so I've had a lot of experience felling trees."

"I must say you found a tree perfectly shaped for that corner. We didn't have to trim a single limb," Teresa replied.

As Teresa and Bryan began arranging greenery, Nancy excused herself. "I better get the lights so we'll have time to finish up before the choir comes to practice the cantata."

As Bryan put the finishing touches on an arrangement of evergreen boughs, Teresa stared at him in amazement. Never before had she known a man with such a sensitive sense of beauty. "You're a man of many talents," she laughed. "You make greenery arrangements like a pro."

"I almost am one," he laughed. "My parents ran a flower and gift shop before they retired. I had to help them every weekend when I was growing up."

Teresa smiled. "You must miss them a lot now."

"I do," Bryan replied. "My brothers and sisters have scattered so we're able to get together only during our annual family reunion every July. What about you? Are you going to be with family for Christmas?"

"I wish," Teresa sighed, "but the holiday season is the busiest time at the shelter. Money is often tight, and that makes for domestic troubles. Families are expected to spend more time together, whether they want to or not. Alcohol consumption soars, and so does family violence."

Bryan shook his head. "It's too bad the happiest season of the year has to be tarnished like that."

"Yes, and it's the children who suffer the most." Teresa frowned. "This year it looks like we'll have five children from two different families spending Christmas at the shelter. The mothers must stay away from their husbands at all costs, so I'm planning a big Christmas party for them."

"Do you need someone to play Santa Claus?"

Teresa nearly dropped a lightbulb she was placing in the greenery on the windowsill. "You?" she gasped, trying to control a snicker.

"Sure. Why not? I think it'd be a lot of fun."

"The kids would love it. Could you come about eleven in the morning, then stay for dinner?" Teresa's mind began to race with ideas.

"That would be perfect." Bryan smiled. "Christmas morning services will be over by nine-thirty. That would give me plenty of time to greet everyone, then change into my Santa suit."

The back door of the church creaked shut as Nancy returned from the hardware store. "Sorry it took so long," she said. "The store was extra busy, and I ended up having to wait on customers before I could leave." She paused and surveyed the sanctuary. "That's beautiful," she said. "If I'd known you were doing such a good job without me, I would have taken more time."

"We just make a good team," Bryan laughed as he placed a ladder close to the tree. "Nancy, if you'll hand me the lights, I'll string them for you. If anyone is going to fall off the ladder, it'd better be me instead of either one of you."

Within minutes the church was completely decorated. As Teresa trudged through the snow to her car, she thought, *That was a strange comment. I wonder what Bryan meant when he said we make a good team. He could have decorated the church twice as well without my interference.*

On the day before Christmas, the skies were dark by four-thirty, and the wind began to howl off the Big Snowy Mountains. The snow, which began as light, graceful flakes, was soon descending on Rocky Bluff in blankets. Teresa stayed at the shelter late into the evening, making sure the food for the Christmas meals was ready to be popped into the oven the next day.

The two mothers staying at the shelter had trouble getting their children to bed. Even when they had finally resigned themselves to stay in their beds, the little ones only pretended to be sleeping, hoping they could catch a glimpse of Santa.

Teresa said good-bye at last and stepped out into the blizzard. She swept the snow off her car's windshield, then shivered and shook her head. *It's not worth risking my neck to drive home in this,* she thought. *I might as well stay here for the night. I'll just use the shelter's extra toothbrushes and nightclothes.*

"What are you doing back so soon?" Brenda, one of the women staying at the shelter, asked Teresa as she reentered the building.

"I don't think anyone should go any place in this." Teresa stomped the snow from her boots. "I'll just sleep in the blue room tonight and help you fix breakfast in the morning. It'll be fun sharing the excitement of Christmas morning with the children."

Brenda gazed out the window at the heavily falling snow. "I hope they won't be too disappointed." Teresa heard a note of sadness in her voice. "I didn't have much money to buy many presents."

"I was going to keep this as a surprise for everyone." Teresa smiled. "But I'm not going to be able to keep quiet. Tomorrow I've arranged to have Santa come; then he's going to stay and have dinner with us. He took the names and ages of the children so he'll be bringing a bag of goodies with him as well."

Brenda put her arm around the shelter's director. "Teresa, I don't know how to thank you for all you've done. This is the most miserable Christmas in my life, but you're demonstrating what the real meaning of Christmas is all about. The kids just don't understand why they can't go home. I can't even tell them where home will be."

"These difficult weeks will gradually fade

into the background as your new life unfolds," Teresa assured her. "Next year at this time, you'll be surprised how far you've come."

"You're so positive." Brenda smiled as the director moved toward the hallway. "Good night, Teresa. Have a good rest."

Teresa slipped into a pair of the shelter's flannel pajamas and crawled under a pile of quilts. Sleep soon enveloped her.

Seven hours later, Teresa's eyes slowly opened as she realized she was in a bed at the shelter and that it was Christmas morning. *I wonder who turned down the thermostat?* she mused. *It's freezing.* She reached through the darkness for the lamp and turned the switch. Nothing. She turned the switch the other direction. Nothing. *Oh, no. The power's out.*

Teresa reached in the nightstand drawer and took out a flashlight. She hurriedly pulled on a sweat suit and her coat. Judging by the temperature of the large, two-story building, she knew the electricity had been off for some time. She hurried downstairs and began searching for candles, flashlights, and matches. In the kitchen, she turned on the faucet to start a steady stream of water to keep the pipes from freezing and bursting. She looked over at the large fireplace at the end of the living room. *I wish I'd followed my instincts and bought several cords of wood for the shelter. It's been several years since Rocky Bluff was without power for an extended period of time, but it was bound to happen sooner or later. These poor children are going to be miserable. It's a terrible way for little ones to start Christmas morning.*

Just then Brenda entered the living room wearing her winter coat. "*Brrr,* it's cold. That must have been some storm last night. The drifts in the front yard look like they're over four feet high."

"I could just kick myself for not having firewood available," Teresa moaned. "I was hoping we'd have a reasonably decent Christmas for the kids, and now we can't even keep them warm. If the snowplows don't clear the streets, I doubt if Santa will be able to get here, either."

Louise, the other mother, joined Teresa and Brenda in the kitchen. Her "Merry Christmas" was muffled and unenthusiastic. Instead of the planned breakfast of ham and Denver omelettes with toast, Teresa served cold rolls, lukewarm orange juice, and bananas. The children seemed to take the lack of power as an adventure, but the adults bemoaned the inconvenience.

After they had finished eating, the oldest boy wandered into the living room to check the size of the snowdrifts from the large picture window. Suddenly, he gave a loud hoot that brought the others running. "Hey, Santa drives a Jeep Cherokee."

Everyone ran to the front window. A man dressed in a Santa suit took a large bag from the back seat and flung it over his shoulder. Seeing the small faces pressed against the window pane, Santa gave a loud "ho-ho-ho" as he trudged toward the front door.

"Santa, why didn't you use the sleigh?" the youngest girl squealed as she flung open the door.

"My reindeer refused to go out in this weather," Santa chuckled, "but fortunately my Jeep was able to start." He leaned over and opened his bag. "I have some presents in my bag with your names on them."

"It's warmer in the kitchen. Maybe the children would like to open their gifts there," Teresa suggested.

Santa handed three gifts to each child and one to each of the mothers. "Where did you get these?" Teresa whispered to Santa.

"The Harknesses helped me pick them out from their store. They were more than happy to donate to the shelter. They have an excess inventory in the hardware store, and these would be going on sale tomorrow anyway," he whispered back.

While the children happily opened their gifts, Santa and Teresa retired to a corner of the kitchen. "Bryan, how could you come so early? I thought Christmas services weren't going to be over until later."

Pastor Olson watched the children play on the floor with their new toys. "Because of the storm only Dawn and Bob Harkness turned up, and they stayed just a few minutes. They were on their way to get their grandmother. Everyone was very concerned about her being without heat, so Bob had started a big fire in their fireplace and was on their way to get Edith. Dawn just happened to mention that the shelter had a large fireplace that had never been used."

"I should have had the forethought to buy at least a cord of wood for emergencies such as this," Teresa lamented.

"Hindsight is always twenty-twenty," Bryan reminded her, "but I brought some firewood with me. It's in the Jeep. I'll get it and start a fire for you."

He went back out into the snow and hoisted the large box of firewood from the back of the Jeep onto his shoulder. Teresa flung open the door as soon as he reached the front step.

"I suppose you learned how to build a fire when you were an Eagle Scout," Teresa teased as Bryan stomped the snow off his Santa boots. "You always seem to have had some past experience that prepares you for whatever life brings."

"Actually, I *was* an Eagle Scout, but I learned to build the family fire before I was eight," the pastor chuckled. He leaned over and arranged newspapers, kindling wood, then logs in the fireplace. Within minutes a roaring fire was heating the living room, and the children moved close to the fire to play with their new toys.

"We all need to thank Santa," Teresa told the children. They gave him a round of applause, and the littlest ones hugged him. The children were even more thrilled when Santa sat on the floor and played with them.

"Don't you have other presents to deliver?" one of the boys asked.

"Nope," Santa chuckled. "This was my last stop, and I'm exhausted. I hope you don't mind my hanging around for awhile."

"We'd love to have you stay for dinner," Teresa said, wondering how Santa could transform back into Pastor Bryan Olson. "But if the power doesn't come on soon, I won't be able to cook the turkey and all the trimmings."

"No problem at all," Santa replied. "We'll just pretend we're on a camping trip. Do you have any hot dogs in the freezer?"

"Sure, we have plenty of those," Teresa replied. "We also have plenty of potato chips, buns, and ketchup."

"Do you have any wire coat hangers?" Santa asked.

"There's some extra ones in the closet in my bedroom," the oldest boy volunteered. He ran to his room to retrieve them.

The women scouted through the kitchen looking for food that could be cooked over an open flame, while Santa entertained the children in the living room. Teresa had envisioned a traditional Christmas meal, and considering other possibilities was hard. The insightful magic of Santa, however, began to fire her imagination. An hour later they had moved the dining room table close to the fireplace and begun arranging their Christmas dinner.

Santa motioned for everyone to join him around the fireplace. He placed the two smallest children on his knees. "Do you know why we celebrate Christmas?" he asked them.

They looked at each other with bewilderment. "It's fun to get presents," one said.

"Do you know what the best present of all is?" Santa asked.

All the children shook their heads. "The best present doesn't come in Santa's sack," Santa said. "The best present was given to us by God. The best present was a baby called Jesus."

All the children listened attentively as Santa told the story of the very first Christmas. When he finished, he made an exaggerated movement of looking at his watch. "Oh, I almost forgot that Mrs. Claus was expecting me home by one o'clock. I'm going to have to be going. I hope you all enjoy your dinner. Merry Christmas to each one of you." With that Santa winked at Teresa, disappeared out the door, and got into his Jeep. Everyone waved as he backed out of the driveway.

"I can hardly wait to tell everyone at kindergarten that Santa stayed and told us the story of the very first Christmas," one of the girls exclaimed as she ran to her mother. "I don't think anyone will believe me."

Just as everyone was voicing their agreement, the doorbell rang. Teresa hurried to answer it. "Pastor Olson, so nice you could come," she greeted as he winked at her. "I hope you'll enjoy our Christmas dinner over the fireplace. That's the best we could do without electricity."

"I wouldn't miss this for anything," Pastor Olson replied as he stomped the snow from his boots and entered the living room.

"Where did you leave your car?" Teresa whispered.

"The Jeep's around the corner. I left my Santa suit on the backseat," he whispered back. "I hope none of the neighbors saw me taking it off. It might disillusion any believing four-year-old child."

Just as they sat down to eat, the power came back on. Everyone cheered, but one of the children looked disappointed. "Does this mean we'll have to stop our camping-out Christmas?"

The adults exchanged amused glances. "I'm not going to give up this hot dog," Teresa laughed. "It's the best one I've ever had."

Pastor Olson stayed and played with the children and their new toys. Then he helped the women carry the leftover food back to the kitchen and returned the table to its proper place. While the others washed dishes, Brenda took the younger children upstairs to bed.

"Mommy, this was the best Christmas

ever. I didn't even miss not being in our house," the youngest one said as Brenda leaned over and kissed her good night. "I hope Santa comes and plays with us again next year."

"It was a Christmas we'll remember for a long time," Brenda replied as she tiptoed out of the room.

Downstairs the phone began to ring. Teresa picked up the receiver. "Hello?" A worried expression spread across her face as she listened to the voice on the other end. "What's wrong, Dawn?"

"I think Grandma had another heart attack," Dawn sobbed. "She's having trouble breathing. The ambulance is on its way. I think it was just too much for her to sit in her cold house for several hours, then have to walk in the deep snow from our car to the house."

"Oh, no. I hope it's nothing serious." Teresa looked up and met Bryan's concerned gaze. "Pastor Olson is here right now. We'll meet your family at the hospital. Just remember, God still has everything under control."

"Teresa, what happened?" Bryan asked as she returned the phone to its cradle. "You look like you've lost your best friend."

"Not yet," Teresa replied sadly. "But she's

mighty ill. That was Dawn Harkness. She thinks Edith may be having another heart attack. They're waiting for the ambulance to arrive. I told her that you and I would meet them at the hospital."

"Has Edith had heart trouble before?" Pastor Olson asked as he put his arm on Teresa's shoulder.

"She's had chronic heart trouble since she had a massive coronary thirteen years ago. She tried to make the best of a bad situation after her last heart attack, and she married Roy Dutton in spite of her limitations. She's an outstanding woman and has been an inspiration to all of us."

"Get your coat," Bryan said gently. "The Jeep can get through the snowdrifts better than your car. I want to be waiting at the hospital when the ambulance arrives." He sighed. "I know Edith is in God's hands, but this is no way to celebrate Christmas Day."

# CHAPTER 5

The minutes passed slowly for the Harkness family as they paced the halls of the Rocky Bluff Community Hospital. They had totally forgotten that this was Christmas Day.

"Dawn, use the pay phone down the hall and call your aunt Jean. Let her know that your grandmother's in the hospital." Bob rubbed his hand across his face and looked around the ER waiting room. "Tell her not to venture out on these roads. We'll keep her advised on Mother's progress. Oh, and call your brother."

"I wish Aunt Jean could be here," Dawn sighed as she rose to leave. "It's nice having a nurse for an aunt. Remember when she stayed with Grandma after her last heart attack?"

"Where does Jean live?" Pastor Olson asked Bob as Dawn left the room.

"She's the head nurse at the new hospital

clinic in Running Butte," Bob explained. "Her husband, Jim, runs the Harkness Two Hardware Store."

Pastor Olson encouraged Bob to talk about his family, trying to help him forget his worry. "Isn't Running Butte on the edge of the Indian reservation?"

"Yes, it's about a hundred miles north of here." Bob watched his daughter drop a quarter into the pay phone down the hall. "Jean helped organize the medical center and spent months cutting through federal regulations. The locals were extremely grateful and made her an honorary member of their tribe."

Pastor Olson leaned forward. "She sounds like a tremendous person."

"She is," Bob replied. "Jean's much like her mother. Always putting others before herself. She's always counseling someone or praying for them."

While the two men talked quietly, Teresa sat close beside Nancy, holding her hand. "The Harkness clan has spent a lot of time at this hospital through the years." Nancy tried to relax in spite of her anxiety about her mother-in-law. "Rural health care has always been a problem for Montana, but Rocky Bluff is fortunate to have this hospital with three doctors. I don't know what we'd do without it."

"I remember when Edith had her first heart attack," Teresa said. "If it hadn't been for the fast action of Dr. Brewer, she would never have survived to become Mrs. Roy Dutton. That was truly a marriage made in heaven." Teresa sighed.

Nancy's smile relaxed the tense lines on her forehead. "Their autumn love was an inspiration to many other couples, both young and old. The Harkness clan was thrilled to include Roy in the family," she said softly. "We were crushed when he had to spend his last year in a nursing home after his stroke. He'd become such an important part of our lives."

Dawn's lower lip trembled when she returned to the waiting room. "Aunt Jean said she and Uncle Jim will drive to Rocky Bluff in the morning. They haven't gotten the roads cleared that far out. But Jay and Angie said they'll be right over. Everyone was shocked that Grandma was sick again. I guess we all got lulled into thinking she was indestructible."

"Edith's faith in God is indestructible," Teresa reminded her, "but her body has gradually gotten weaker and weaker."

"I couldn't stand to have her in a nursing home like Roy," Dawn said with tears in her eyes. "I'd quit work and stay with her twenty-four hours a day."

"I agree," Nancy stated firmly. "After what happened today, your grandmother cannot live by herself any longer. We can always remodel the den and have her move in with us. She'll be right at home since it was originally her home for nearly forty years. It wasn't until after her first heart attack that she decided the house was too big for her to care for any longer. When she and Roy married, they chose to live in his house because it was the smaller of the two houses. But it's time for her to come back home."

The Harkness family and Teresa shared with their new pastor the impact that Edith had had on the family and the entire community. They told of her bravery in disarming a distraught high school student while she was still teaching home economics in Rocky Bluff High School. They told of all the people she had helped while she was a volunteer at the crisis center. They enjoyed telling how she met and fell in love with the director of the center, Roy Dutton. With each passing anecdote, Pastor Olson was amazed that one woman could have accomplished so much in one short lifetime. *Edith sounds like the model virtuous woman the Bible talks about in Proverbs,* Pastor Olson thought.

Just then a cold wind blew across the hospital waiting room. Glancing up, Dawn saw her brother and sister-in-law shaking snow from their boots. "Jay!" she exclaimed as she ran to embrace him. "I'm so glad you came."

"How's Grandma doing?" Jay asked as he hugged his younger sister.

"We haven't had any word," Dawn replied grimly. "She looked terrible when the ambulance brought her here. Her breathing was so shallow."

Jay and Angie turned to greet the others, then found chairs next to Dawn. Their presence seemed to lift the cloud of anxiety that hung over Dawn. "It's going to be all right, Sis," Jay said as he patted her hand. "God has taken good care of Grandma for all these years. He's not going to let her down now."

Dawn's eyes settled on a water spot on the carpeting. "Grandma's always been there every time I've needed prayer support," she murmured. "I don't know what I'd do without her."

"I guess it's time we all start depending on our own faith in God instead of relying solely on Grandma's prayers," Jay replied solemnly.

"That's easy for you to say," Dawn protested. "You've always been strong and in control of your life. Look what a mess I've made of mine."

Jay shot a panicky look at the others. He couldn't think of what he should say. After a long silence, Teresa was the first to respond. "Dawn, I think you're selling yourself short. Strength comes from God. You can't manufacture it yourself."

Pastor Olson marveled at Teresa's theological perception. Rarely had he seen such depth of spiritual understanding, even in the seminary he had attended. Yet here in small-town Montana where the common, ordinary people lived out their lives, Christian faith and wisdom abounded.

Suddenly, Dr. Brewer appeared in the doorway, and everyone jumped to their feet. "How is she?" Bob asked.

"She's stabilized now, and I think she's going to make it," the doctor replied as he motioned for everyone to be seated. He took the chair next to Bob and pulled it a few inches closer to the others. "From all indications her heart has been further weakened, but she seems to be holding her own. We're going to move her to intensive care so we can monitor her tonight, but I expect tomorrow she can be moved to a private room."

A deep furrow creased Nancy's forehead. "What's her long-term prognosis?"

"We can't be sure for a few days, but my guess is she will be much weaker, and walking will become even more difficult for her," Dr. Brewer explained. He had spent many hours with the family through the years, and he knew he could speak openly and frankly with them. "If I were you, I'd invest in a wheelchair for her as soon as she's discharged from the hospital. I also wouldn't recommend her living alone any longer."

"I couldn't bear to have her in a nursing home like Roy was," Jay said.

Dawn nodded her head in agreement. "We discussed that before you got here," she explained. "We're going to remodel the den and put her bed and dresser there."

Jay rubbed his chin. "That's where she had her bedroom after her first heart attack when she could no longer climb stairs. She always loved that room. It's so light and airy."

Dr. Brewer stood to leave. "If you'd like to spend a few minutes with Edith before she's moved to intensive care, you may do so. Just remember, she is still very weak."

The Harkness family, followed by Teresa

and Pastor Olson, tiptoed into the emergency room where Edith lay connected to an oxygen tank and several monitors. They each spoke to her, though she scarcely responded. Pastor Olson led the family in a quiet prayer of comfort and healing, and they all went softly from the room. They all had lumps in their throats, and Dawn could not hold back her tears.

The family said good-bye to each other and made plans when each would return to the hospital. Jay and Angie headed across the snowy parking lot to their car; Bob, Nancy, and Dawn went the other direction; and Pastor Olson and Teresa walked to the pastor's Jeep.

"This has definitely been an eventful Christmas," Bryan said as he opened the door for Teresa. "From blizzards, to playing Santa Claus, to preparing dinner without power, to being involved in a crisis with one of the most faith-filled families I have ever met. There never seems to be a dull moment in Rocky Bluff."

Teresa mulled over Bryan's words as he scraped the ice from the windshield of the car. As he slid behind the wheel, she said, "Montana is a land of contrasts. You never know what's going to happen next, but there's one thing you can be assured of: In a crisis, all Montanans pull together."

The next morning, Bob slipped out of bed before the sun was up and headed for the bathroom. Hearing the shower running, Nancy rolled over and looked at the illuminated clock. She waited for her husband to return. "Bob, it's your day off. Why are you up so early?"

"I want to get to the hospital as soon as possible," Bob replied as he reached in the closet for a clean shirt. "The last time Mother was ill, I dumped her on Jean. I figure now it's time for me to do my part."

Nancy nodded in agreement as she remembered how Bob had been determined to put his mother in a nursing home instead of being responsible for her care. Edith's first heart attack had caused Bob to do a great deal of soul searching, and he was now a changed man.

"Even if you're there, I bet Jean will still hover over her mother," Nancy chuckled. "Once a nurse, always a nurse." Nancy got up and wrapped a robe around her slim waist. "I'll fix you a hot breakfast before you go."

"That's not necessary," Bob replied as he finished buttoning his shirt. "I'll get something later. I want to check on how Mom did through the night."

Nancy combed the tangles from her hair. "Call me as soon as you know anything," she replied. "In the meantime, I'll start clearing out the den for her. Jean and Jim and the girls are planning on leaving Running Butte first thing this morning so they should be here by ten o'clock. I'll ride to the hospital with them."

Bob brushed his lips across Nancy's as he hurried out the door. "See you later. Don't work too hard. I'll do the heavy stuff when I get home."

The snowplows had worked most of the night, and the major streets were now passable. Bob did not lose any time driving to the hospital. He went directly to the intensive care wing and greeted the head nurse. "How's my mother doing?"

"She had a good night and is resting comfortably," the nurse replied. "I'm sure the doctor will move her to a private room some time today."

"If she's awake, may I see her?" Bob asked.

"I'm sure she'd like that." The nurse nodded for him to enter the room near the end of the hall. "She should be waking soon."

Bob thanked the nurse and made his way quickly to his mother's room. As he opened the door, Edith turned her head and opened her eyes. "Hi, Bob. What are you doing here so early?"

"I just wanted to check on how you were doing."

"I'm a lot better today. Sorry I messed up your Christmas." She smiled weakly.

"You didn't mess it up as much as the snow and power outage did," Bob chuckled. "It's good to see you looking so chipper. Sounds like you'll be moved to a private room later today."

"I'm glad of that." Edith's face became serious as she hesitated, trying to choose exactly the right words. "I don't think I'll ever be strong enough to live by myself again," she stated matter-of-factly. "Would you check to see if there will be any openings in the nursing home soon?"

Bob's eyes scolded his mother as he took her hand. "We'll do that only as a last resort. Right now Nancy is cleaning the den so you can have it as your room again. She and Dawn will take turns caring for you."

"But I don't want to disrupt your family life," Edith protested. "You all have jobs to tend to and lives to live."

Bob shook his head and smiled. "You know from all the years you and Dad ran the store that winter is the slowest time of year. This will give me a good excuse to cut back Nancy's and Dawn's hours without hurting their feelings."

"Bob, quit teasing," Edith replied as her normal twinkle returned to her eyes. "I know full well what you're trying to do. I appreciate your offer, though."

Edith hesitated. She needed several minutes before she could come to terms with the dramatic change about to occur in her life. A look of resignation spread across her face. "Maybe we could give it a try for a few weeks and see how it works out. Do you think someone could help me move my bed and a few clothes to your den?"

Bob patted his mother's hand. "Believe me, you'll be overwhelmed with help. Jean and Jim are on their way to Rocky Bluff now, and of course Jay and Angie will be happy to help."

Just then the door opened, and a nurse's aide came in carrying a breakfast tray. "Ready to eat, Mrs. Dutton?"

"I'm very hungry," Edith replied. "I missed out on the big Christmas dinner last night."

"Looks pretty good for hospital food," Bob laughed as he turned to leave. "I wonder if they have something similar in the cafeteria for me to eat."

■ ■ ■ ■

Teresa awoke early and groaned as she looked out the window at the heavy snow-drifts in the front yard. *One disadvantage about being single,* she sighed. *I have to shovel my own snow or wait two days before one of the neighbor boys has time.* She pulled on a pair of sweats and hurried to the kitchen where she ate a breakfast of oat-meal and hot chocolate.

Taking a parka and boots from the hall closet, she bundled herself against the cold elements. When she opened the door, the harsh, subzero temperature numbed her face. She found the snow shovel in the garage and began shoveling the front side-walk. By the time she was only halfway to the street, tears were running down her cheeks. *I'll never get this finished. And even if I do, then I'll have to go to the shelter and see that it's dug out. I wish I'd contracted for snow removal, but I hated to spend the money. I thought since we had so much snow last year we'd have an open season this winter. That was so stupid of me. Montana weather is totally unpredictable.*

Teresa stuck her shovel in the snow and leaned on it to rest. A familiar Jeep Cherokee stopped in front of the house. "Do you need some help?" Bryan shouted.

"You better believe it," Teresa yelled back. "I'm kicking myself for not having a snow-removal contract."

"Well, how about going inside and putting on a fresh pot of coffee? I'll have this done in no time." Bryan opened the back of the Jeep and took out a snowblower.

Teresa watched from the kitchen window as Bryan not only cleared the snow from the sidewalk but the driveway as well. When he was finished, he turned off the snow-blower and headed for the front steps. "Come in and warm yourself," Teresa greeted as she flung open the door. "You must be freezing."

"I am," Bryan replied as he sank into a kitchen chair, "but doing your driveway didn't take nearly as long as doing the driveway and sidewalks at the shelter."

Teresa's eyes widened as she set a piping hot cup of coffee before him. "You mean you've already been over there?"

"Well, of course," he chided. "You don't think I'd stay in bed all morning, do you? Besides, I thought you might like to come with me to check on Edith Dutton. I've known her only a few days, but after last night, I feel like I've known her a lifetime."

"It'll take me a bit to change clothes and freshen up," Teresa replied. "I hope I won't keep you from doing your pastoral duties."

"Oh, no." Bryan chuckled. "I'm sure your presence will be more healing and therapeutic than mine. There's something about a woman's touch when you're sick."

Teresa poured her pastor another cup of coffee. "Thanks for the vote of encouragement." She smiled. "I'll try to hurry."

Within a half hour Teresa and Bryan were pulling into the parking lot of the Rocky Bluff Community Hospital. As they went inside, Dawn came racing toward them.

"Grandma's a lot better today. They've just moved her to a private room," she said breathlessly. "Let me take you to her."

She led the way down the wide hospital corridor. "We're going to move her bed over to our den this afternoon. The doctor says she'll be out of the hospital in a couple of days so I'll have a chance to take care of her. Maybe that way I'll be able to make up for all the terrible things I've done."

Pastor Olson opened his mouth, but before he could speak, Teresa put her arm around Dawn and chided lightly, "Where did you ever get your lousy theology? Regardless of how hard you work, you'll never be able to erase your past mistakes. Just

confess them to God and those you've offended; then go on with your life. Jesus has
already paid the price for your sins, so you
don't have to keep beating yourself with
them."

Tears filled Dawn's eyes. "Teresa, you're
such a wonderful person. You always know
just the right thing to say. You're such an
encouragement to me. I don't know what
I'd do without you."

"Probably rely on the good Lord a lot
more," Teresa chuckled as she gave Dawn a
hug.

Pastor Olson fell a few steps behind the
two women but stayed close enough to hear
their conversation. *The ministry of encouragement is the most neglected ministry in all
Christendom, and yet Rocky Bluff is blessed
with both Teresa Lennon and Edith Dutton as
encouragers. I wonder if they've studied
Barnabas's relationship with the Apostle Paul?*

# CHAPTER 6

New Year's Eve was a quiet, uneventful evening but exciting nonetheless for the Harkness family as they gathered in the living room of Bob and Nancy's home. Nancy and Dawn had finished converting the den into a bedroom for Edith. Jean had moved a few of her mother's favorite things from the house Edith had shared with Roy Dutton for nearly ten years, back to the original Harkness family home.

An expression of contentment spread across Edith's face as she relaxed in her wheelchair at the end of the sofa. She watched her two youngest grandchildren lying on the floor, playing with the hand-held computer games they had received for Christmas. Her eyes next drifted to her older grandchildren seated on the sofa. Jay sat tall and handsome, lovingly holding his pregnant wife's hand.

"There couldn't be a better way to usher

in the new year than surrounded by my family," Edith sighed. "Not a single one is missing, and the hope for the coming year is extremely bright."

Everyone nodded in agreement except Dawn, who was lost in her own thoughts. *How can Grandma be so optimistic a week after she nearly died? I wish I had her confidence that next year will be better than the last one. I'd like to go back to college, but I'm afraid I'll make a mess of things again. I know I don't have the strength to stand up to the temptations there and to keep my mind on my work.*

Edith's heart twinged as she noted the pained expression on her granddaughter's face. She tried to avoid drawing attention to Dawn's inner turmoil and focused instead on her granddaughter-in-law. "Angie, will your mother be able to come to Rocky Bluff when the baby arrives?"

"I'm due the end of May," Angie replied. "She's already purchased her round-trip ticket from Guam and will be here from the middle of May until after the Fourth of July."

"This is her first grandchild, and she can hardly contain herself," Jay laughed. "I wouldn't be surprised if she moves to

Montana after she retires from teaching."

"I couldn't think of a better place to retire," Edith replied with a twinkle in her eyes. "There's a lot to do here, and watching grandchildren grow up is worth a major move."

"Take it from the world's greatest doting grandmother," Jean teased. "When I had my first baby, if you'd listened to Mother, you'd have thought Amy was the first baby born in the great Northwest."

Nancy shook her head. "I doubt that," she laughed. "Long before Amy, she let Bob and me think that Jay was the first and greatest child ever born."

Just then the phone rang, and Bob hurried to answer it. "Hello. Yes, Dawn is here. One moment, and I'll get her."

Hearing her name, Dawn hurried to the phone. "Hello?"

"Dawn, I haven't talked to you since early last fall." Dawn recognized the voice of her friend, Tara Wolf. "How have things been going?"

"Fine," Dawn murmured. "I've been keeping busy."

"I'm home from college, and I wanted to see you and catch up on the latest. We're having a big party at Linda Wright's, and all the old gang will be there. Can you come and join us?"

Dawn hesitated. She thought back to the laughs and good times she used to have with her old friends. She remembered the midnight swimming, the skiing races, and the rodeo parties. *Sure, I'd love to,* almost slipped from her lips, but the cell in the Chief Joseph County Jail flashed before her. "I won't be able to come tonight. My entire family is here now, and I'd hate to leave them on New Year's Eve."

Dawn shuddered as Tara snickered. "That never stopped you before. I've never known you to turn down a party. This isn't a big deal. We're just going to get together, have a few beers, have some fun. Why don't you want to come? What gives?"

"Oh, nothing," Dawn retorted. "Grandma just got out of the hospital today. She's moving in with us."

"You mean you'd choose being with your grandmother over being with us?" Tara taunted.

Blood rushed to Dawn's face, and her voice trembled. "Yes, I would."

"If that's the way you want it, I'll see you around." Tara hung up the phone.

Dawn stared blankly out the kitchen

window as she returned the phone to its cradle.

"Is something wrong, Dear?" Edith called from the living room. She watched the stunned expression on her granddaughter's face.

Dawn shook her head and redirected her attention back to her family. "No, I'm fine." She rejoined her brother and sister-in-law on the couch. "That was Tara Wolf. Some of my old friends are having a party at Linda Wright's house tonight, and they wanted me to join them. I turned them down. I'd rather spend New Year's Eve with my family."

Jay beamed and patted his sister on the shoulder. "Atta girl. I'm really proud of you for turning down a party invitation from that crowd. Even when I was in high school, they lived a pretty risky lifestyle. Their parties always seemed to be one step ahead of the law."

"So I found out," Dawn replied, "except it was me who got caught by the law, and not them."

Jay hugged his sister. "You're the lucky one. You're well on the way to normalcy, while they're still wasting the best years of their lives partying."

Dawn sighed and laid her head on her

brother's shoulder. "I wish I was as strong as everyone thought. I'd like to return to college for the spring semester, but I don't think I'd make it. I almost said yes to Tara tonight, even surrounded by those who love me. Without your presence, I'm sure I would have gone to that party and probably ended back in rehab."

"You'll make it, Sis. Just hang in there," Jay assured her.

The rest of the evening the family watched videos and ate popcorn. Even though she was weary, Edith was determined to stay awake until after midnight. Ever since her December 31st wedding to Roy Dutton, every New Year's Eve held a sweet specialness for her. The beginning of a new year was like the beginning of a new life. Even though her body was becoming weaker and weaker with each passing year, her spirit was constantly being restored and refurbished. She was able to sit back and watch the ministry of encouragement, which she had tried to demonstrate for so many years, being practiced by her family and friends. She only wished she was still in the center of the activities in Rocky Bluff.

Teresa slept late New Year's Day. Crisis counseling was emotionally draining for her, and her body ached with fatigue. Whenever a holiday gave an excuse for a lot of partying and drinking, the incidents of spousal abuse skyrocketed. She had been busy most of the night, and two new women and their children were now staying at the shelter.

She stumbled into the kitchen and made herself a cup of instant coffee. As she dropped a couple slices of toast into the toaster, the telephone rang.

*Who can that be? I thought all of the New Year's Eve crises would be over,* she thought as she hurried to the phone.

"Happy New Year, Teresa. This is Bryan Olson."

"What are you doing up and about so early New Year's morning?" Teresa chided.

"I've been at the hospital most of the night," Bryan replied solemnly. "There was a group of young people who were partying last night, and it got totally out of hand. The mixture of bad drugs and alcohol caused the death of one girl, and another is in critical condition. A third is in satisfactory condition."

Teresa's face blanched as her knuckles whitened around the phone. "Who are they? Nobody local, I hope."

"I'm afraid so," Bryan sighed. "A young woman named Tara Wolf died, Linda Wright is in critical condition, and Marsha Harris is recovering and could be discharged later today. The pastors of the parents of Tara and Linda are with their families, but Marsha's parents live in Wyoming. I tried to help her the best I could and contacted her parents for her. They're on their way from Sheridan now."

"How awful," Teresa gasped. "Is there anything I can do?"

"That's why I called. I think Marsha needs a woman's hand to hold until her mother gets here. She's extremely distraught."

"I just woke up. Give me at least forty-five minutes." Teresa glanced in the hall mirror and frowned at her disheveled hair and the bags under her eyes.

"I'll be by to pick you up in about an hour," Bryan replied. "I was sure I could count on you to help me out. There are times when a woman's touch can accomplish more than all my years of seminary training."

Marsha Harris lay sobbing on her hospital bed when Teresa tiptoed into the room. She rolled over when she heard the door open and forced a faint smile. "Hello," she murmured.

"Hi." Teresa approached the bed. "My name is Teresa Lennon. Pastor Olson said you might like some female company until your mother gets here."

"It would beat staring at the ceiling," Marsha sighed as she took a tissue from the box and wiped her eyes. "I feel so alone and scared. Last night was a nightmare."

"What happened?" Teresa pulled up a chair next to the bed.

"It all started as an innocent party, but by midnight things had gotten out of hand. At first we were just enjoying a few drinks; then some guys from Billings turned up with drugs that weren't supposed to have any lasting effects. Now look at us. Tara's dead . . . Linda's in critical condition . . . and my father has told me that if I were ever involved in drugs again he'd completely disown me."

"If you level with your father and go through drug rehabilitation, don't you think he'll forgive you?"

"He's pretty hardheaded," Marsha said, "but underneath he's got a tender heart. It all depends on which side of him prevails."

Teresa took the young woman's hand. "Most fathers are like that. I'm sure he'll come around."

"I know," Marsha sighed. "I only wish I

had the strength that Dawn Harkness had. Do you know her?"

A small grin spread across Teresa's face. "I've been a friend of the entire family for years."

"She's lucky," Marsha replied. "She chose to stay home with her family on New Year's Eve instead of going to the party. Tara begged her to come, but Dawn insisted that her family was more important. I wish I had a flawless family like that."

Teresa shook her head and gave a dry smile. "Dawn's family is definitely not problem-free. In fact, at times I wonder how they have withstood all the tragedies they have had, but their faith in God is equal to any hardships they've had to face."

Marsha's eyes began to brighten, but she hesitated for several moments. "I heard rumors that Dawn went through the drug rehab in Billings. Is that true?" she asked shyly.

Teresa paused, not wanting to betray any confidences that Dawn had shared with her. However, she knew how burdened Dawn had become about her friends still using drugs. "She completed treatment right before Christmas. I'm sure she'd be willing to talk with you about it. She's becoming a real crusader for a drug-free society."

"Maybe I'll talk to her later," Marsha replied. "Right now all I want to do is go back to Sheridan and forget I've ever been in Rocky Bluff. Maybe in a few days I'll feel like giving Dawn a call and talk about going to rehab myself. If it did that much for her, maybe it would help me too."

"Rehab is an excellent recovery method," Teresa said as she watched the interest increase in Marsha's eyes. "However, Dawn had something else going for her to give her strength."

"What was that?"

"Dawn turned to God, and she found that He was always there to help." Teresa paused, fearing she might be minimizing the inner struggles Dawn had experienced. "It hasn't always been easy for her, but through this long ordeal Dawn discovered God's forgiveness and love even when she felt alone and rejected. It was extremely liberating for her to find God not only on the mountaintops but in the valleys as well."

Tears began to stream down Marsha's cheeks. "You know, I used to go to Sunday school when I was a kid," she confessed, "but when I got in high school, church seemed so silly and only good for little old ladies who were getting ready to die. I didn't think it would have anything to offer me.

Now look at me. I have absolutely nothing, plus one dead friend and another who may not live. I don't have anything."

Teresa handed Marsha another tissue and waited for her to dry her eyes. "That's just where God wants all of us," Teresa explained. "He wants us to quit relying on our own strength and turn to Christ for our strength."

The two were still in deep conversation an hour later when Pastor Olson appeared in the doorway with a smile on his face. "Marsha, how are you feeling?"

"Better, thank you."

"Well, I have some good news for you."

"What's that? I need something good to happen," Marsha murmured.

"They just took Linda out of the intensive care unit and upgraded her condition to stable. She's going to be all right."

Marsha heaved a sigh of relief. "That's wonderful."

At two o'clock that afternoon, Marsha's parents arrived at the Rocky Bluff Community Hospital and signed the necessary release papers. Pastor Olson said good-bye to the family with a prayer and received an assurance from them that they would call if there was anything he could do to help.

After the Harrises disappeared across the parking lot, Bryan turned to Teresa, "I haven't eaten since breakfast. How about joining me for lunch at the Hamburger Shack?"

"Sounds good, but I don't want to stay too long," Teresa replied. "I want to touch base with Dawn and let her know what happened before the gossip gets around town. At one time she was extremely close to the kids at that party."

"Why don't we call Dawn and see if she can join us?" Bryan suggested. "I'm sure we can find a quiet corner this time of day."

"Give me a minute, and I'll call her from the pay phone in the lobby." Teresa reached in her purse for a quarter.

Bryan sunk into an overstuffed chair in the lobby while Teresa made her call. He admired her soft brown hair that she had pulled back with a bow to match her blouse. *Teresa always looks so nice, and she knows how to handle the most sensitive issues. It's going to be interesting to see how she breaks the bad news to Dawn. If it were not for Dawn's family and Teresa's encouragement, I doubt if Dawn would have had the strength to say no to the party. She could be lying in the hospital herself.*

■ ■ ■ ■

Forty minutes later the threesome huddled in a back booth of the Hamburger Shack with hot chocolate and hamburgers in front of them. Dawn looked from Bryan to Teresa and back again. A wrinkle spread across her forehead as she saw their strained faces. "Judging by your expressions, you didn't invite me to lunch to discuss the weather. What's going on?"

Bryan and Teresa exchanged glances. "Dawn, did you hear what happened at Linda Wright's party last night?"

Dawn's face blanched as she shook her head. "No," she replied. "How'd you know there was a party?"

"We just left the hospital after having been there several hours," Bryan explained sadly. "Tara Wolf, Linda Wright, and Marsha Harris suffered drug overdoses. Marsha was just released. It was touch and go with Linda, but they finally upgraded her condition and removed her from intensive care by noon."

Bryan hesitated as Dawn's eyes widened. "What about Tara?" she begged. "Is she going to be okay?"

Teresa reached out and took her young friend's hand. "I'm sorry. They weren't able to save her. She died early this morning."

"She can't be dead!" Dawn slammed her fist onto the table. "They were only going to do a little drinking. She told me so when she called and invited me to the party."

"Marsha says a couple of young men came from Billings with some bad drugs," Teresa replied. "They told those from Rocky Bluff that the drugs would not have any lasting side effects."

Dawn's face reddened as she again slammed her fist onto the table. "I hate them. They killed my best friend. I hope they rot in jail." Her voice was shaking uncontrollably.

Teresa rubbed Dawn's shoulder. "You have every right to be angry. Giving drugs to others is one of the cruelest forms of inhumanity, but you can't let yourself become consumed with hatred. It will only destroy you and will never work for any good."

For the next ten minutes, Dawn sobbed while Teresa and Bryan sat in understanding silence. Gradually the sobs became further and further apart until they finally ceased. "I almost went to that party. I could easily have been the one lying in the morgue instead of Tara. I'll never go to another wild party as long as I live. A few minutes' high isn't worth dying."

Bryan and Teresa waited for Dawn to sort out her emotions. Finally, a resolute gleam appeared in the young woman's eyes. "God must have spared me for a reason. I'll do whatever I can to convince others not to use drugs."

# CHAPTER 7

Dawn Harkness surveyed the eager faces that filled the auditorium of the Rocky Bluff Middle School. Eight years before, she had been sitting in one of the same seats, listening to returning graduates tell about their college experiences. However, Dawn's message was not about selecting a major, attending college classes, or cramming for finals. Instead, she was talking about the temptations of alcohol and drugs.

"Last week I buried one of my closest friends," Dawn said, and a hush spread over the room. "A group of my friends were partying, thinking only of having fun, without considering the consequences of their behavior. I know, because until a few months ago I would have been partying with them. Oh, we had all heard of people overdosing on drugs, but we never thought it would happen to us." Dawn paused as she noticed a large boy with peach fuzz on his face wiggling uncomfortably in his seat. "Would any of you like to guess why I am standing before you now instead of being in the cemetery with my friend?"

The silence that had settled over the room grew more intense. The students leaned forward in their seats. Finally the boy with the peach fuzz murmured, "You must have been lucky."

"Yes, I was very lucky," Dawn agreed. "A few months ago I got caught using drugs and went to jail. So I wasn't at the party where my friend lost her life."

"That doesn't sound very lucky to me," the boy snickered.

"As strange as it may seem, the night I got busted was the luckiest night in my life. It scared me straight. It forced me to accept the fact that I had a problem and had lost control of my life. Only then was I willing to go through rehabilitation."

With that honest confession, Dawn was able to share the physical and emotional effects that drugs had had on her body. She shared the loneliness of going through the rehabilitation program. She told of the love and support her family and the people of Rocky Bluff had shown her during this difficult period. After her talk, Dawn passed out cards and asked the class to join her and sign their names to a pledge promising to refrain from all forms of substance abuse.

Every pair of eyes was glued to the floor. No one moved. *I've failed,* Dawn moaned silently. *I've poured out my heart to them for nothing. I'll never speak to another group of students again. Teresa said that sharing what happened to me and encouraging others not to go down the same path would strengthen me in my commitment, but it's not true. I'll never do this again as long as I live.*

"Why is everyone just sitting here?" the boy with the peach fuzz exclaimed. "I don't want to end up in jail, rehab, or the cemetery. I'm going to join Dawn and promise to remain drug-free." He hurriedly scribbled his name on the bottom of a pledge card, walked to the front of the room, and handed it to Dawn. One by one, all the others followed his lead.

Tears gathered in Dawn's eyes. *Teresa was right, after all,* she thought. *If I can keep just one other young person from using drugs, the humiliation of retelling my story will make it all worthwhile.*

Teresa Lennon gazed out her office window. The trees were beginning to bud. The winter had been long and hard, with an overabundance of tragedies and heartaches, but the new leaves brought the hope of springtime.

Teresa leisurely flipped through the day's mail. *Just imagine the number of trees that had to die to produce all this junk,* she sighed. The one letter in the pile that caught her eye had the return address of the Drug and Alcohol Abuse Center in Great Falls. She hurriedly tore it open.

You are invited to a one-week seminar on identifying and assisting drug abuse victims, sponsored by the United States Department of Health, Education, and Welfare. Please complete the enclosed registration form and return it before March thirtieth.

Teresa finished reading the enclosed brochure. She recognized the main speaker as a nationally renowned authority in the field. *After all my experiences with Dawn these last six months, I sure could use more training.* She immediately filled out the registration form, wrote a check for the registration fee, and placed them in an envelope.

Just as Teresa licked the envelope, the

telephone rang. "Hello, Spouse Abuse Shelter. This is Teresa. May I help you?"

"Hello, Teresa. This is Bryan. I haven't heard from you in several days. I was wondering how things were going."

"Life has been pretty quiet around here lately," Teresa replied as she leaned back in her chair. "I think the death of Tara Wolf had a sobering effect on the entire community."

"It definitely had a sobering effect on me," Bryan admitted. "Ministering to so many people who were directly or indirectly connected to the drug party was mind-boggling to me. I feel that I'm not trained to minister to that kind of social problem. I worked with drug addicts in Boise, but I always felt so inadequate."

"You're being too humble," Teresa encouraged. "I heard many positive comments about how much help you were to them."

Bryan shook his head. "People were very supportive, but in my heart of hearts, I knew that I should have been able to do more."

Teresa shuffled through the papers on her desk. "I just received something in the mail that might be of interest to you. There's a week-long seminar in Great Falls coming up in April on identifying and helping victims of drug abuse. It's put on by the

United States Department of Health, Education, and Welfare. They're bringing in some pretty high-powered speakers. I just sealed the envelope with my registration fee."

"Sounds interesting. Mind if I go along?"

"Please do," Teresa replied. "Since Rocky Bluff is no longer immune to drug abuse, the more of us who receive this training the better equipped we'll be to cope with the problems."

After a long pause on the other end of the line, Bryan finally responded. "Do you know if anyone else from Rocky Bluff is going?"

"I don't know of anyone," Teresa replied. "Like I said, it just came in today's mail. Why do you ask?"

"One thing I've learned in my early years of ministry is to avoid even the appearance of impropriety. If it got around that you and I went out of town for a week together, I'm sure it would set tongues to wagging."

Teresa smiled ruefully. "I'm afraid you're right. That's the downside of living in a small town . . . the local gossip mill. As a pastor you're more susceptible to it than the rest of us."

"I am well aware of that," Bryan sighed. "I know several God-fearing ministers whose reputations were tarnished because of idle gossip and misunderstandings."

Teresa thought a moment. "Maybe I could call the guidance counselor at the high school and see if she's interested in going."

"Just don't ask her to go along as a chaperon," Bryan snickered. "I don't want to feel like a sixteen-year-old boy again."

"I'll be discreet," Teresa chided back. "I'll also make a copy of the brochure and the registration form and get back to you later today or tomorrow."

As the two bade each other good-bye, Teresa felt a warm flush spread across her face. *Bryan seems much more interested in me than in his other parishioners.* That moment of ecstasy was soon followed by concern. *I wonder if Bryan would be as interested in me if he knew my background? I so enjoy our times together, but I'm afraid I'll become too attached and will be hurt again if he ever finds out about my past.*

She shook her head sharply as if to erase all bad memories and walked to the kitchen to refill her coffee mug. Too many people with more serious problems were depending on her; she didn't have time to spend considering her own emotional needs. Returning to her desk, she took out the phone book and looked up the number of the Rocky Bluff High School. Moments later the call was transferred to the counseling office.

"Hello. This is Valerie Snyder."

Teresa explained about the seminar, and Valerie was enthusiastic about going along with Teresa and Bryan. "I just have to have my principal approve my leave time and expenses. He's generally pretty agreeable about additional training."

Valerie cleared her throat. "Not to change the subject, but I just spoke with one of the middle school teachers. She said Dawn Harkness spoke to the students earlier this afternoon about how drugs nearly destroyed her life. She was a smashing success, and everyone in the auditorium signed a pledge promising to live a drug-free lifestyle. Dawn has a tremendous message."

Teresa smiled. "Dawn has come a long way. If it hadn't been for her family, I don't know if she could have come through this difficult time of her life."

The conversation drifted to lighter topics, then they said good-bye. Teresa had just hung up the phone when it rang again. "Hello. Spouse Abuse Shelter," she replied mechanically.

"Hi. It's me again," Bryan Olson chuckled. "I was just thinking that a nice juicy steak would sound pretty good for dinner tonight. Would you like to join me at the Steak House?"

Without hesitation Teresa replied, "I'd love to. I'll bring the copy of the seminar brochure with me, and we'll talk about it there."

"Great. I'll pick you up at seven," Bryan agreed.

Something in his voice as he said goodbye made Teresa feel nervous and giddy. Afraid to acknowledge her feelings, she left her desk and began cleaning the already immaculate kitchen. She tried to mentally plan the next meeting with the volunteers, but her mind kept drifting back to the handsome pastor who seemed to be slipping into every facet of her life.

That evening after finishing a filet mignon, Bryan and Teresa leisurely sipped their coffee as they enjoyed their dessert. They discussed the upcoming seminar, and Bryan agreed to drive his car to Great Falls. They discussed current events at the national level and locally. Everything was light and superficial.

Then Bryan became serious. He studied Teresa's deep green eyes. "Teresa, I've known you for five months now, and underneath your deep compassion for others, I sense a hidden story that needs to be shared. How did you happen to get into working with spouse abuse cases?"

A distant gaze settled on Teresa's soft face. The moment she had feared was upon her. Would her background cool their friendship? Teresa took a deep breath. "I once had to take advantage of the services of the spouse abuse shelter in Missoula."

"I'm sorry to hear that." She could see nothing in his face except sympathy. He leaned toward her. "You seem to have turned tragedy into triumph. Would you care to tell me what happened?"

Again Teresa took a deep breath. "I've never talked much about it. Mine is such a strange story. Are you sure you want to hear it?"

"Only if you care to share it." Bryan reached across the table and took her hand.

Teresa flushed as she nervously twisted the corner of her napkin. "My husband was a respected marriage counselor who lived a double life. At home he was totally different than he was in public. Although he was outwardly a Christian, it was all a sham. He was subject to —" She bit her lip, looked quickly at Bryan, then away. "Fits of rage," she finished. "Soon after we were married, he began to verbally abuse me. He soon escalated to physical violence, though he was careful to leave bruises only where they could not be seen."

Her voice was very low now. "When I could no longer take the physical and emotional abuse, I called a spouse abuse shelter. They were extremely helpful and encouraged me to move to the shelter for a few days to get through a crisis. I'll always be grateful for what they did for me."

A furrow deepened on Bryan's forehead. "So what did your husband do when he discovered you were gone?"

Tears filled Teresa's eyes. "I had thought he would be upset and would try to get me back. I thought he would be willing at last to get counseling. But he merely moved in with the woman he had been seeing on the sly. It wasn't until after I had left that I learned the extent of his adulterous relationships."

Bryan squeezed Teresa's hand. "That must have hurt. Rejection like that . . ." He shook his head, and she saw her own pain reflected in his face. Then he grew very still, and though he still held her hand, his grip loosened. He looked down at the table. "Are you still married to him?" he asked hesitantly.

Teresa sighed. "I was raised to believe that divorce was unthinkable, and yet I was faced with a reality I couldn't escape. I knew the Bible said adultery was grounds for divorce, but I had trouble accepting it."

Bryan let go of Teresa's hand and leaned back. He carefully folded his napkin. "I share your feelings about divorce. How were you able to decide what to do?"

Teresa shook her head. "I didn't have to decide anything. I had no say whatsoever in what happened next. He divorced me and married the 'other woman' six months later. They moved to the East, and I picked up the pieces of my life. I felt that in God's eyes I was still married, and so of course I shut myself off from relationships with other men. I felt as though I had reached a dead end in my life. I couldn't see where I was supposed to go next."

Teresa sighed. "Somehow, even though I was the victim, I carried a cloud of guilt around with me for many years. Just admitting that I was a divorcée was more than I could bear. I took very seriously the Scripture that said divorced women should not remarry, and I refused to develop even a friendship with any man."

Bryan looked up at her. "You didn't have any trouble developing a friendship with me." He looked at her questioningly. She could still see the kindness in his gaze, but the warmth was more distant, as though he had put up a wall between himself and her.

Teresa picked up her coffee cup and looked down into it. "My circumstances are different now," she said softly. "You see, I'm a widow now, not a divorcée. Not that that made any difference to me for a long time. I'd been hurt so badly that I just wasn't interested in being close to a man in any way." She looked up at him and smiled shyly. "But you were different. You kind of slipped in through the back door. Circumstances kept throwing us together, and I couldn't resist your friendship."

Bryan let out a long sigh. "Your husband died?"

"That's the tragedy of it all," Teresa replied. "Five years after he left me, he found out he had cancer. His new wife refused to nurse him. I suspect he had abused her also. She moved back to Montana, and he died alone, a broken man. However, before he died, he made peace with God. He wrote me a letter telling me about his illness and his conversion, and he begged me for my forgiveness." She smiled faintly. "It was a very strange experience. In a way, he had died for me years before when I accepted he no longer loved me. And yet I had remained faithful to him, had stayed married to him in my own mind and heart. So I grieved when he died . . . and yet I couldn't share my sorrow with anyone, because no one here knows about my past. I was sorry I never got to see him again. I never even got to tell him that I forgave him gladly. By the time I received the letter, he was already dead."

"At least you have the assurance that he did make his peace with God before he died," Bryan reminded her.

"That's true," Teresa said.

Bryan looked at her face. "Why didn't you remarry then?" he asked gently. "After all, when your husband died, in God's eyes you were free to marry again. I know you'd been hurt, but after all those years God must have brought healing to your heart. Otherwise you wouldn't have been able to minister so effectively to others who were hurting. Someone as caring . . ." He smiled, and added, "and attractive as yourself. I'm surprised no man entered your life in all these years."

Teresa hesitated. "You're right. After my husband died, I did feel free to remarry.

But by then I was so busy with my career. I had been single long enough that dating just wasn't part of my lifestyle. I was just too immersed in the lives of those who came through the doors of the shelter. All the people of Rocky Bluff have become my family." She met his eyes. "I never felt the need for anyone else." *Until now,* something whispered inside her.

"Rocky Bluff may be your family," Bryan said, his voice soft, "but if you've never shared your past, then you've kept part of yourself separate and alone. I feel honored that you have shared that part of your life with me."

Teresa leaned forward and smiled at her pastor. "It is rather liberating to be able to talk honestly with someone without feeling that underneath I'm hiding something."

She set down her coffee cup and sighed. "My husband's counseling office was in our church, so when I lost my husband, I also lost the church where I was a member. I couldn't go back there. No one knew the true story, and many blamed me for the breakup of our marriage. It caused an extremely intense spiritual struggle for me. I knew it wasn't God's fault, but I couldn't understand why things had happened the way they did. I had tried so hard to save my marriage, but I hadn't felt God wanted me to stay and be beaten any longer. I still hoped our marriage would be healed, even when I was at the shelter. You see, when I went to the shelter, I never thought I was walking away from my marriage. I just knew I needed help."

She sighed again. "I had loved being active in the church. I always loved working with the children and the women's Bible study groups. But suddenly it was over, and I was out in the cold. I vowed I would never get actively involved in a church again but would remain by myself in the back pew."

She smiled. "Gradually, Edith Dutton was able to get me involved again. Other than you, she's the only one in Rocky Bluff who knows I was once the wife of a church marriage counselor."

"Your secret is safe with me," Bryan assured her. "But I'll bet you were a tremendous counselor's wife. I'm surprised that anyone would have rejected you." He looked into her eyes. "It wasn't your fault, Teresa. You did all you could. Someday maybe you'll not feel ashamed to talk more freely about your past."

# CHAPTER 8

Teresa, Bryan, and Valerie Snyder relaxed over late-night desserts in a diner down the street from their hotel. The conference on drug addiction and intervention had been exhausting; yet no one was ready to retire. They needed time to process the day's load of information.

"That was a provocative session tonight," Valerie noted as she laid her fork on her empty plate. "It was an eye-opener for me that drug abusers have trouble talking about their problem. Most of the kids I work with are pretty open about their situations. They want to talk, and they're just looking for someone to listen. But the people we learned about today —" She broke off and shook her head. "I can't imagine living a life with a hidden secret."

Teresa shifted nervously in the booth. "Sometimes people are afraid of being rejected," she said as her gaze drifted across the restaurant's dark windows. "Life can get so complicated. . . . It's hard for people to understand another person's problems unless they have experienced them themselves. That's why there are support groups for every known problem imaginable."

"From that aspect, I can understand a certain degree of privacy," Valerie agreed. "If a person felt that others were judgmental, he'd be bound to pull into his own shell. It must be dreadfully lonesome to carry a private secret, afraid to share your pain with anyone."

Teresa and Bryan exchanged glances. "It is," Teresa said solemnly. "I can speak from experience."

Valerie studied her friend's face. "Not you?" she gasped, unable to mask her surprise. "You're one of the most all-together people in Rocky Bluff. I can't imagine the Rock of Gibraltar having some hidden past."

"There's a lot about me that people don't know. I've spent years trying to mask my pain," Teresa replied. "I was hoping I was doing a good job."

"Believe me, you did an excellent job of hiding your feelings," Valerie said, "but has it been worth it?"

"At times I wonder." Teresa's eyes moved

blankly from the windows to the salt shaker on the center of the table. "It wasn't until I met Bryan that I realized how foolish I'd been. He helped me understand that people accept me for who I am, not for what has happened to me."

Bryan took Teresa's hand and looked into her face. "Teresa, that's the first time I've heard you admit that masking your feelings was not the best way to live."

"You've been a big help," Teresa sighed. "I didn't know how relaxing life could be until you moved to Rocky Bluff and became my pastor." She tightened her jaw to keep back the other words she longed to say.

Valerie smiled at her older friend. "Pastor Olson has been a comfort and guide to many of us in Rocky Bluff. I'm sure nothing in your past would have been a shock to him."

Teresa and Bryan again exchanged glances. "He wasn't shocked," Teresa agreed, "but he had to admit it was highly unusual for a marriage counselor to be traveling the country with his wife, giving marriage seminars while he was having extramarital affairs on the side."

Valerie gulped, trying hard not to react. "You mean you were the wife? That must have torn you to the quick. How did you ever adjust?"

"I don't think I ever did," Teresa replied. "When I learned about Chris's behavior, I was devastated. I had already tried everything possible to try to keep him. I had let him subject me to all kinds of physical and emotional humiliation. I thought I had to live up to our public image." Teresa paused, and a tear glistened in the corner of her eye. "Nothing I tried worked, and he left me for another woman in spite of all my noble attempts."

"He must have been a real jerk," Valerie stated firmly. "How could you have stayed with him as long as you did?"

"Everything I'd been taught since I was a child emphasized the importance of saving a marriage at all costs, especially since we were presenting ourselves as a model couple. Divorce was something that happened to other people, never to me."

"None of us are immune to heartache," Valerie reminded her. "You are so compassionate to the failures of others. . . . Why couldn't you accept divorce for yourself?"

Teresa shrugged her shoulders. "I must have thought I could do superhuman feats on my own strength without relying on God's grace and support," she replied. "That's how foolish I had become."

Valerie turned her attention to the man beside her. "Pastor, isn't adultery considered grounds for divorce?"

Bryan nodded his head. "Yes, in fact it's the *only* biblical grounds for divorce. But human emotions run deep, and every situation is different. Some marriages are healed even after abuse and adultery. We have a God who is able to work miracles of healing when we commit ourselves to doing our part. But when one spouse hardens his heart and leaves, there's not much the other can do."

"I felt that although Chris had remarried I should remain single the rest of my life," Teresa told Valerie. "Just because he had broken his marriage vows didn't mean I couldn't remain faithful to mine. However, three years ago Chris died of cancer. I'm ashamed to say this, but in the midst of my grief I also felt liberated, no longer tied to a dead marriage." A faint smile curled the corners of her lips. "However, I think I've been single too long and am too set in my ways to start over now." She shrugged her shoulders and slumped deeper in the booth.

"After watching the changes in Edith Dutton and Rebecca Hatfield after they remarried in their later years, I'd say autumn love must be sweeter than first love," Valerie noted as she yawned and glanced at her watch. "I think I'd better call it a night and get some shut-eye."

The three paid their bills and walked slowly to Bryan's Jeep. The wind whipped around their heavy coats and tousled their uncovered hair. The late-night desserts had relaxed their bodies and emotions, but a faint uneasiness hung over Teresa. *Will an autumn love be possible for me?*

When they arrived at the hotel, Valerie said good night and turned down the long corridor toward her room. Bryan took Teresa's hand. "You look troubled. How about finding a corner of the coffee shop for a little true confession?"

Teresa blushed. "You mean my feelings are showing?"

"No, I'm just a good mind reader," Bryan chuckled as he led the way to a corner table.

After the waitress served two cups of hot tea, Bryan studied the lines on Teresa's soft face. "I was proud of you tonight. I know it was difficult for you to share the pain of your past."

"In this situation it seemed to come naturally," Teresa replied.

"I think Valerie's opinion of you grew tremendously when she realized the inner strength it took to go through what you did," Bryan replied.

Teresa shook her head. "I don't think I should be admired just because I've been through a lot of pain."

"You didn't let the pain embitter you," Bryan replied. "You drew upon it to develop true character. I just hope you haven't hardened yourself against ever marrying again."

Teresa gave a faint laugh. "I've never given it much thought. I've been too busy trying to help others in crisis situations."

"I think it's about time you think of Teresa Lennon once in awhile. Teresa deserves to love and be loved as much as those who come to the shelter do."

Teresa blushed, then hesitated, trying to choose her words carefully. "If I'm not being too personal, why did you never marry? Did you not want to love and be loved?"

"I asked for that," Bryan chuckled. "I was engaged once . . . back when I was in seminary."

"What happened? Did she leave you for someone else?"

A pained smile spread across Bryan's face. "I think I could have accepted that better," he sighed. "There are a lot of guys out there better looking and with greater personalities. The reason she left me was because she didn't think she'd be able to cope with the pressures of being a minister's wife."

"You mean you had to choose between her and your calling to serve God in the public ministry?"

Bryan nodded his head. "You put it very well," he replied. "I almost dropped out of my last semester of seminary. In fact, I was halfway across the campus toward the registrar's office with my withdrawal form when it hit me. . . . I had to put God first in my life."

"Do you know what happened to her?" Teresa asked.

"The last I heard, Sherry had married a computer engineer and has three children. Since she left me, I've been afraid to ask any woman to live her life under the ministry's close community scrutiny."

"In a little town everyone lives under close scrutiny," Teresa laughed. "Our former pastor's wife seemed to thrive on the opportunity to serve the community. She just laughed if someone hinted she didn't quite fit the stereotype of a proper minister's wife."

"That's one thing you definitely need in this business," Bryan replied with a twinkle in his eyes. "A good sense of humor."

Teresa took another sip of her tea and replaced the cup in its saucer. "How true that is," she replied, "but it's not much different from being the director of a spouse abuse shelter."

"Teresa, I've been encouraging you to take down your barriers for weeks. Now it's my turn to admit the softening of my own shell," Bryan said as he gazed into her eyes. "I do feel lonely and need someone to share my life. After I met you, I began to reveal parts of my life that I'd never shared with anyone. The feelings I have for you are different from what I've felt toward anyone else. It's entirely different from what I experienced with Sherry years ago."

Tears gathered in Teresa's eyes. "The attraction is mutual. Even during the good times of my relationship with Chris, I never shared as much as I have with you. It's like I'm entering into new and uncharted waters. I think I like it, but I'm afraid I'll be hurt again or make a fool of myself."

"Then let's go slowly," Bryan replied gently. "I love you, and I'm looking forward to charting unfamiliar waters with you. We both will need to do a lot of soul-searching to adjust to the smoldering coals within us. My guess is that those embers of attraction are going to ignite into a steady flame . . .

something that may warm us for the rest of our lives."

Teresa blinked the tears from her eyes. She felt both frightened and elated at the same time, but she looked away from Bryan's intent gaze, afraid she'd say something she'd regret later. She did not want to either commit herself to more than she was ready for or push him away. "Perhaps," she replied at last, her voice light, "but in the meantime, I think I'd like to get some sleep. The morning session is going to be starting too early."

Bryan wrapped his arm around Teresa's waist as they walked down the corridor to their rooms. When they got to Teresa's door, she took her key from her purse and turned to say good night. Bryan took her firmly in his arms and pressed his lips against hers.

Teresa's pulse began to race. She had long since forgotten the ecstasy of being held and loved. "I love you," he whispered. He let go of her reluctantly. "If I'm not careful, those burning embers I told you about are going to burst into roaring flames." He smiled ruefully.

"The feeling is mutual," Teresa replied, her voice shaking. She turned the knob and slipped into her room.

Valerie was sleeping peacefully in the far bed. Teresa flopped across her own bed with her mind in a whirl. *Is this for real? Am I really falling in love? Is Bryan really falling in love with me? I feel more confused than a teenager.*

When the conference ended at the end of the week, every participant raved about the knowledge they had gained and planned how they would apply this new information to their particular situation. The effects of this conference were going to be felt all across the state, but most particularly in Rocky Bluff, for Bryan Olson and Teresa Lennon had learned something besides techniques for counseling drug abusers. They had learned something about each other, and they had each admitted the growing love between them.

Her first morning home, Teresa leaned back in her kitchen chair and sighed. *I'm just too tired to tackle the mountain of work that has accumulated at the shelter. I'll give Edith a call and see if we can share a cup of coffee.*

Within minutes, Teresa and Edith were seated at the Harkness kitchen table. Nancy, Bob, and Dawn were at work so Edith had the entire house to herself. Her mind was as alert as ever, and she listened with a keen interest as Teresa told her the details of the conference and how they were going to use that information to help those in Rocky Bluff.

Teresa shifted in her seat. "Now, what's happened in Rocky Bluff while we were gone?"

Edith smiled and shook her head. "I guess the most exciting thing is that Bob has a new employee at the hardware store, and the town is really humming. Gabriel Brown is an Afro-American from South Carolina. He's an expert at repairing farm machinery, but the community definitely didn't put a welcome mat out for him and his family."

"Why not? We have people moving in and out of town all the time."

"But this is the first black family to move to Rocky Bluff." Edith spoke with a new intensity. She shook her head. "I must say I'm both surprised and dismayed by the town's reaction. After all, ten percent of our population is Native American, and Angie Harkness is a Pacific Islander. But we've never had Afro-Americans before." Her lips pressed together. "I'm ashamed that anyone in Rocky Bluff cares what color a person's skin is."

Teresa shook her head. "As much as we'd like to think Montana is an island unto itself, I guess we're not immune from the social problems the rest of the world has to face."

"The part that concerns me the most is that Gabriel and Mandy Brown have an eleven-year-old son named Nathan. Most of the kids at school have accepted him, but several have begun taunting him with racial epithets."

Teresa wrinkled her brow. "Has the school done anything about it?"

"The principal called the entire student body to the gym and told them there would be severe repercussions if anyone is caught using racial slurs or discriminating against someone of another race," Edith explained.

"Do they think it did any good?" Teresa asked.

"It may have stopped it at school, but until you change people's attitudes, the problems will persist," Edith replied. "There's evidence that racial prejudice is not limited to kids on the playground."

"What else is going on?" Teresa queried, not believing that racial prejudice could be in their sleepy town.

Edith shook her head with disgust. "Last night racial threats were spray-painted on the Browns' garage. This is more than a children's prank and will be treated by the police as vandalism and a hate crime."

"Do they know who did it?"

"Police Chief Philip Mooney is working on it, but so far they don't have much to go on. However, the word is around town: Rocky Bluff will not tolerate racism nor permit vandalism. The new motto is: Not in our town."

"I have all kinds of confidence in our police and fire departments," Teresa replied. "After all they've dealt with in this town during the last years, I'm sure they can find and punish these vandals."

"Chances are it's a bunch of kids." Edith sighed wearily. "The school's keeping its ears open."

"Good. Valerie never misses anything that goes on in that school," Teresa replied. "After spending a week with her at the conference, I'm even more impressed with her than I ever was."

Teresa glanced at her watch and noted the slump in Edith's shoulders. Concern mounted each time she visited her older friend, for Edith seemed to be weaker than the time before. Teresa realized how heart-breaking it had been for her to give up her home and move in with her son and his family after all her years of independence. "Edith, before I go, would you like me to fix you a sandwich and a bowl of soup?"

Edith took a heavy breath. "I'd appreciate that," she sighed. "They're so busy at the store lately; I don't think any of them are planning to come home for lunch."

Teresa went to the refrigerator and surveyed its contents. "What would you like me to fix? There's some cheese here in front. Would you like a grilled cheese sandwich?"

Edith nodded her head. "Sounds good. I think there's probably a can of tomato soup in the bottom left-hand cupboard."

Teresa glanced back at her older friend. "Why don't you go lie down while I fix lunch? I'll let you know when it's ready."

"Thanks," Edith replied, her voice hardly above a whisper. Edith then walked cautiously to the living room, holding onto the wall and pieces of furniture as she went. She closed her eyes as soon as she stretched out on the sofa. Teresa had followed her into the living room, and she gently spread an afghan over her. Edith drifted off to sleep.

Twenty minutes later, Teresa had a light lunch arranged on TV trays for Edith and herself. An artificial flower arrangement graced the kitchen table so Teresa gently removed one blossom and placed it on Edith's tray. Going an extra step for such a saintly woman was the least she could do.

As she set a tray beside the sofa, Edith

opened her eyes and looked around. "Oh . . . I must have dozed off," she said as she reached for her glasses on the end table. "The tray is beautiful."

Teresa said a short prayer of thanksgiving, and they ate their lunch in relaxed silence. They were used to not only sharing their words but also their quiet times, and they found peace in each other's presence. After they ate, Teresa did the dishes, while Edith stretched out again and was soon fast asleep.

*I better get to the shelter and see what's going on,* Teresa told herself. *I hope there weren't any crises while I was gone.*

But as soon as she opened the door to the shelter, Mary Evers, one of the volunteers, came bounding toward her. "Teresa, am I glad to see you," she gasped. "Can we go to your office and talk?"

"Sure," Teresa replied as she motioned for her to follow. "What's up?"

Mary dropped into a chair. "The night before last a man living up Hunter Creek Road went berserk and held his family captive for three hours before the sheriff's deputies could talk him out. He's still in custody, but they brought his wife and the children here."

"I'm glad to hear they're here," Teresa replied. "That's what we're here for. How are they doing? They must be terribly traumatized."

Mary shook her head. "They are. The mother has stayed in her room, crying for twenty-four hours straight. I can scarcely get her to eat. Her name's Michelle Frank. I hope you'll be able to help her."

A deep furrow creased Teresa's forehead. "I'll go and talk with her and see what I can do. What about the children? How are they doing?"

"Richie is ten and Chuck is twelve," Mary said as she sunk deeper into her chair. "They're in school now, but they're absolute monsters when they're here. I don't know how we're going to deal with them. They don't have any relatives to turn to so I feel like we're on our own with a couple of uncontrollables."

"I'll talk with the counselor at the school," Teresa said. "I'm sure we'll be able to do something to help those poor children."

Mary shook her head in disbelief. "It won't be easy."

# CHAPTER 9

Teresa collapsed onto her sofa. She mindlessly reached for the TV remote and flipped through the channels. Nothing caught her attention, and as the phone rang, she flicked the remote's off button.

"Hello," she wearily greeted.

"You sound tired." Bryan Olson's voice was deep with concern. "How are you doing?"

"I'm exhausted," Teresa replied. "The best part of my day was this morning when I visited Edith Dutton, but even that was a little depressing because she's continuing to fail. I wish I could do something for her. She's such a sweet and loving person."

"I agree," Bryan replied. "I don't think we could find a more perceptive and compassionate person in Rocky Bluff . . . unless her name is Teresa Lennon."

Teresa blushed. "I could never live up to her standards," she sighed. "In fact, I've

142

spent the entire afternoon with a family problem that is way over my head."

"Would you like to talk about it?" Bryan asked. "As a pastor you can count on my confidentiality . . . and as a friend you need someone to lean on."

Teresa leaned her head against the back of the sofa. "It would be nice," she sighed, "but I'm sure you're just as tired as I am."

Bryan laughed. "Of course I'm tired, but it's time we put away our superficiality. Let's be tired together. We've got to quit playing super-helper and admit our need for each other's support. I'll be over in half an hour."

After she hung up, a new surge of energy raced through Teresa, and she hurried to the bathroom. She plugged in her curling iron and added fresh makeup while it heated. By the time Bryan arrived, Teresa was dressed in a crisp blue jumpsuit. She looked as fresh as she had at the beginning of her day.

After fifteen minutes of small talk, Bryan took Teresa's hand in his. "Enough chitchat. Now tell me what the real problem is."

A dam seemed to break inside Teresa, and she poured out the feelings of inadequacy she had experienced while dealing with the traumatized Frank family. As the words tumbled out her mouth, the intensity of her feelings surprised her. "I think I was able to communicate with Michelle," she explained, "but I feel completely helpless with the boys. After talking with Valerie about their behavior at school, I found out that things were even worse than I thought. I don't know what we're going to do. Not only are they defiant at school, but they are completely insubordinate at the shelter. The volunteers are suspicious they are sneaking out after everyone is in bed, but they haven't been able to catch them yet. I can't expect my volunteers to stay up all night guarding the doors."

"Maybe we should talk to Chief Mooney about the situation. I'm sure his police officers don't miss a thing when they're out on night patrol."

"Bryan, why didn't I think of that myself?" Teresa smiled at him. "In the big cities the police are so overworked with murder and mayhem they'd never be able to help with trivial problems. At least in Rocky Bluff, the police have the time to practice preventive crime control."

They agreed on a time to go to the police station; then they changed the subject to a more relaxing topic — the anticipated arrival of Jay and Angie Harkness's baby. Since his bride was a beautiful Chamorro girl from Guam, everyone was anxious to view the most beautiful baby ever to have taken a breath in Rocky Bluff.

But after Bryan left that night, a melancholy mood settled over Teresa as she thought of the arrival of Jay and Angie's baby. Teresa had long ago accepted her life of singleness, but now the thought of having a baby of her own to love and nurture overwhelmed her. If only it were possible. . . . She knew her biological clock was ticking loudly, and to consider having a child after the age of forty was probably unreasonable. *I wonder if Bryan has ever missed having children?* she thought. *He would make an ideal father and role model.*

The next morning at ten o'clock, Bryan and Teresa were seated in Police Chief Philip Mooney's office expressing their concern about the Frank family. Chief Mooney explained the legal status of the father who had been sent to a mental institution for psychological evaluation and treatment.

"I'm concerned about his wife and children," Teresa said. "Michelle is extremely emotional, and the boys seem to be getting themselves in all kinds of trouble. The volunteers are suspicious that the boys might be sneaking out at night. Would it be possible for your night patrol to keep a watch on the shelter for any unusual happenings?"

The police chief leaned back in his chair. "I wonder . . ." He scratched his head. "Those boys just might be the guilty parties we've been looking for. The night before last, the garage of the new African-American family was spray-painted with racial epithets. Last night, Rocky Bluff's Native American families were the spraypaint targets. Judging by the spelling, it has to be children. I wonder if they're taking their frustrations out on the rest of the world. We'll surely keep an eye out for any unusual activities around the shelter."

Bryan and Teresa thanked the police chief for his help, then walked hand in hand back to Bryan's Jeep. As he started the engine, Bryan turned to Teresa, "Would you like me to drop you at your home or at the shelter?"

Teresa hesitated. "That's a tough choice. I have desks piled high with work in both places. Maybe I better clear off my desk at home first."

Arriving at Teresa's home, Bryan walked her to the door. "Hang in there," he said as he took her in his arms. "I'll be praying for you. Don't try to carry the burden of the entire community on yourself. The Lord will see that everything works out for the best."

The warmth and assurance of Bryan's embrace calmed Teresa's nerves, and the tension lines on her face began to fade. "Thanks," she whispered. "Just knowing there's another human being who understands and supports me means so much. I truly understand now what the Bible means about us all being one church, functioning together as a single body." She smiled up at him, her eyes shy. "Thank you. Thank you for showing me that I can depend on someone . . . that it's not just me and the Lord all by ourselves."

Bryan's lips melted over Teresa's, while their souls seemed to entwine. The pressures of the present and the uncertainties of the future faded in that moment of union. They were each finally convinced that they would share the rest of their lives together.

Teresa had just finished booting her computer when the doorbell rang. *Who could that be?* she sighed as she hurried toward the door. *I hope everything's okay at the shelter.*

Her face spread into a broad grin as she

opened the door. "Dawn, come in. How are you doing?" Teresa gave the young woman a warm hug.

"I'm doing fine, but things aren't going as well for Angie," Dawn replied.

"Take off your coat and tell me what's going on. Is there a problem with the baby?"

"There could be." The pair seated themselves on opposite ends of the sofa. "She and Jay just got back from the doctor's, and there is a good chance she could go into premature labor. The doctor wants her to remain bedfast for the remaining six weeks of her pregnancy."

"That's going to be hard," Teresa said.

"I know," Dawn replied, "but Angie's determined to do whatever is necessary to give that baby the best chance it can possibly have. But Jay's really concerned about Angie being by herself while he's at work. He asked me to move in with them until the baby comes."

"That's a good solution. I hope everything works out for all of you."

"There's one big problem," Dawn explained with frustration. "Dad's new employee, Gabriel Brown, and his family are very uncomfortable with the racial tension that seems to be developing in Rocky Bluff. If there's one more incident of graffiti, they're planning to move back to South Carolina. If they leave now and I have to be with Angie all day, Dad will be short of help. He's already putting in too many long hours as it is. Do you think the police will find out who's doing all this graffiti and put a stop to it soon?"

Teresa took a deep breath and paused. She wanted to calm Dawn's fears, but she knew the police had no proof, only strong suspicions. "Pastor Olson and I talked with Chief Mooney this morning," she said carefully. "Hopefully they'll have a handle on this in a few days."

"I guess all we can do is take one day at a time." Dawn shook her head with frustration. "I'd hate to have the Browns leave town. I've really enjoyed getting to know them."

The two chatted for another half hour; then Dawn left to pack her clothes to move into Jay and Angie's spare bedroom. Teresa returned to her computer and stared blankly at the screen. *Why do all the crises in Rocky Bluff have to come at the same time? The community has barely calmed down from the dreadful drug party New Year's Eve, and now they're faced with this. It's curious. Whenever something happens in this town, the Harkness family is somehow involved. I guess if you live on the cutting edge like they do, you're going to be impacted by the sins and frailties of others.*

Just as Teresa was leaving for the shelter the next morning, the telephone rang. She hurried back to answer it. "Hello?"

"Teresa, you've got to come right away," a frantic voice cried.

"Dawn, is that you?"

"Yes. Teresa, you've got to come and help me."

"What's wrong?"

"Someone has spray painted the words, 'Go back to your little grass shack,' on the side of Jay and Angie's garage. Angie's hysterical. I'm afraid if she doesn't calm down she'll lose the baby."

"I'll be right there," Teresa promised as she hung up the phone.

She paused, then dialed a familiar number. As soon as she heard Bryan's voice, she explained what had happened.

"Oh, no," Bryan said. "When is this ever going to end? I'll stop by and talk to Chief Mooney, then join you there. I'll be praying the entire way."

"Thanks," Teresa replied. "We all need it."

■ ■ ■ ■

For the next two hours, Teresa talked with Angie and Dawn. Little by little, Angie's sobbing stopped, and she grew calm. Teresa fixed everyone soothing cups of herbal tea, and the mood of the three turned to levity. However, during Dawn and Angie's string of silly jokes, Teresa became more and more restless. *Where's Bryan?* she wondered. *He said he would be right over. It's not like him to let me down. Fortunately, Angie was able to get ahold of herself before anything serious happened. I don't know what I'd have done if I couldn't calm her. I suppose I would have had to call an ambulance. Isn't that just like a man — make a promise, then not follow through? I suppose something must have come up.*

Just then the doorbell rang, and Dawn went to answer it. "Pastor Olson, Chief Mooney, do come in."

"How's Angie?" Pastor Olson asked as Dawn led them into the living room where the pregnant woman was lying on the sofa.

"I'm doing better," Angie replied. "I feel silly for having come apart the way I did. I think my hormones are all out of balance."

"You needn't apologize," Bryan said as he

pulled up a footstool next to the sofa beside her. "Your reaction was perfectly under-standable under the circumstances. We have some good news for you." He glanced at Teresa who was sitting in the chair at the end of the sofa. "We solved the mystery and apprehended our graffiti artists."

Teresa leaned forward in her seat. *How could I have possibly questioned Bryan's reli-ability?* she thought ruefully.

"Who was it?" Angie asked as she propped herself up with the pillows.

"Two brothers ages ten and twelve who are staying at the spouse abuse shelter. They will come by in a few days with a paintbrush and remove their damage." Pastor Olson's words were for Angie, but he kept his eyes on Teresa.

"So it *was* them." Teresa sighed. "How did you figure it out?"

Chief Mooney stepped forward. "While we were driving down the alley behind the shelter, Capt. Packwood spotted a pile of spray-paint cans. We went to the school and talked with the boys. They both had black paint all over their hands. They admitted what they had done pretty readily."

Teresa shook her head in disgust. "What happens to the boys now?" She looked from

Bryan to the chief of police.

"We've had a long talk with the boys, their mother, and the school officials," Bryan replied. "I think we've come up with a temporary solution."

"What's going to happen to them?" Angie asked. "The kids must be scared to death."

"The mother is having a lot of emotional problems adjusting to what has happened, so she has agreed to admit herself to the psychiatric ward in the Great Falls hospital. Hopefully, she'll experience a good quick recovery and will be able to return home and care for her family," Pastor Olson explained. His eyes settled on Teresa's concerned face before continuing. "While she's in the hospital, I've agreed to have the boys stay in the parsonage with me. I'll supervise the boys while they repaint all the buildings in Rocky Bluff that they've vandalized. The school counselor will work extensively with the boys while they're at school."

Teresa smiled. "That's so generous of you. You'd make a great father figure."

Bryan shook his head and grinned at Teresa. "I'm headed into uncharted waters again. I'm going to need all kinds of support."

After everyone had finished discussing the ramifications of the latest calamity that had struck Rocky Bluff, Teresa, Pastor Olson, and Chief Mooney excused themselves, leaving Angie to get some rest. As soon as they were outside, Bryan turned to Teresa. "Since I came in the police car, would you mind giving me a ride home?"

"No problem at all," Teresa responded as they turned toward her car.

"I'm famished. How about stopping at the Uptown Restaurant for lunch?"

"Better yet," Teresa said as she started the engine, "would you like to come to my house for lunch? I have a home-cooked casserole in the freezer, and it would take only a few minutes to microwave it."

"I'll take home-cooked meals any time," Bryan laughed. "Besides, we have some personal planning to do. I've never been a father before, and these boys are going to need a substitute mother until their own mother is better."

# CHAPTER 10

Bryan Olson perched himself on the stool at the counter while Teresa prepared lunch. The kitchen's homeyness melted any remaining hesitation he'd felt about surrendering his bachelorhood. *Why have I wasted all these years? I wish I'd met her years ago. My spiritual life did develop when I had no one to share my life with except my Lord, but I need a soul mate now to share my struggles and dreams.*

They sat down, and Bryan said the blessing. They ate in silence, but the quiet was companionable rather than awkward. At last, Bryan laid his fork on his plate and sighed. "Teresa, I don't know if I'm up to what I just committed myself to. I've never been a father before."

Teresa nodded. "Every new parent feels the same way. Everyone wants a child to come with an instruction manual."

Bryan sighed again. "I'm the one who preaches about walking by faith, but when I'm confronted with uncharted waters, I'm the first to panic."

Teresa chuckled as she recognized her own failings in Bryan's words. "I'm willing to panic with you. I haven't had much experience with preadolescent boys myself, but I'm willing to help all I can."

"Okay, then let's plan our strategy." Bryan squared his shoulders. "As soon as the boys move into the parsonage, I'll take them around to all the people they've offended, have them apologize, then set up a time when they can repaint the garages and sheds they defaced."

"Do you know how many buildings are involved?"

"At the last police count, there were fifteen, so they're going to be a couple of busy boys for several months."

"That's the best way to keep them out of trouble," Teresa replied, "but we'll also need to get them involved in long-term activities." She paused thoughtfully. "They've lived in the woods most of their years, and their socialization has been minimal. They rode the bus to school in the morning and went home directly after school, so they never had an opportunity to participate in any of the extracurricular activities the other kids did."

"The Boy Scouts are active here," Bryan suggested. "It might be good to encourage them to join. I think Scott Packwood is the troop leader." His enthusiasm mounted. "Speaking of socialization and moral training, every Wednesday after school we have a group of children meet at the church. They call themselves the King's Kids. Everyone I've talked to is impressed with the group."

"The King's Kids sounds like a good idea. Also, Little League season will be starting in six weeks," Teresa noted. "I know Jay Harkness coaches one of the teams. Maybe we can get the boys interested in that."

Bryan chuckled. "If all goes as planned, we'll have the boys so busy they won't have time to get into trouble."

"That's the main idea." Teresa laughed. "Every Saturday when the new TV schedule comes out we can sit down with them and plan the programs they'll view for the week. We can even help them decide which videos they want to rent that week. That ought to be a real treat since they didn't have access to a TV while they were living in their cabin in the woods."

Bryan gazed into Teresa's soft green eyes. "We sure make a good team, don't we?"

Teresa flushed. "Sure do. Neither one of us could do this alone." She hesitated, realizing the magnitude of their undertaking. "When were you planning to take charge of the boys?"

"This Saturday. I'm planning to drive their mother to the hospital in Great Falls. The doctors want to meet with the children at that time. Saturday would also be a good time to take them shopping. It ought to be fun furnishing their rooms. We can give them a fair amount of liberty when it comes to decor. Money and good taste would be their only limiting factors." He glanced up at her quickly. "Would you be able to come to Great Falls with us?"

Teresa's eyes brightened. "Sure. It'll be great fun buying the boys new clothes and helping them plan their bedrooms."

Bryan moved his chair closer to Teresa's and took her hand, pressing it to his lips. "While we are in Great Falls, we can also pick out a diamond ring for you."

"A what?" Teresa gulped.

"A diamond ring," Bryan replied calmly. "Teresa, I love you, and I want to share the rest of my years with you. I hope you feel the same about me."

Teresa laid her head against his shoulder. "I love you more than I ever thought possible. I can't imagine spending the rest of my life without you. I've been alone for so many years that I didn't realize how much I was missing until I met you."

"You're not afraid of being a pastor's wife, in spite of all the challenges that accompany it?" Bryan was tormented by the twenty-year-old memory of rejection because of his vocation.

"I once thought a pastor's wife had one of the most difficult jobs anyone could have," Teresa confessed. "But now I've decided that if I could live in the public eye as wife of a prominent marriage counselor, I can easily face the challenges of being a pastor's wife in Rocky Bluff, Montana." She hesitated. Her background too came back to haunt her. "But what if someone questions you about marrying a divorced woman?"

Bryan's face reddened. "After I told them to mind their own business," Bryan paused, recognizing the level of his anger. He took a deep breath. "I would gently explain that your divorce was your ex-husband's idea, not yours, and that since then he has passed away. As a widow, you are free to remarry. I admit that people can be very cruel at times, but when Christians face objections with love and understanding, obstacles can be overcome."

"I've lived in Rocky Bluff a long time now, and I've learned one thing about its people," Teresa replied. "Occasionally they react to a situation without thinking, but in the end, this is probably one of the most supportive communities anyone could find."

Bryan took Teresa in his arms. Silence enveloped the pair as years of unacknowledged loneliness melted. "Then you will marry me?" he pleaded. His voice was hesitant, as though he could barely believe his good fortune.

"Yes," she whispered, tears filling her eyes.

"If we buy the ring Saturday, may I announce the good news to the congregation Sunday?"

"Are you ready to handle a congregation that may faint when they learn that two confirmed singles, who have never shown an interest in the dating game before, now plan to marry?" Teresa chuckled.

Bryan leaned back his head and laughed. "I'll have to deal with that when it happens. I suppose there will be a lot of shocked expressions. I think most people thought we were merely interested in the same public service projects and never noticed our lingering glances."

Teresa's smile widened. Never before had she known the love and assurance she felt when she was in Bryan's presence. "I'll be proud to proclaim our love to the entire world."

The next few days flew by for Teresa. She helped Bryan rearrange the two back bedrooms in the parsonage. She registered Chuck and Richie in the Boy Scouts and checked into the Little League schedule. She helped their mother organize her business affairs for her absence during her hospital stay and spent hours listening to Michelle pour out the pain of years of abuse. Teresa's thoughts of her recent engagement were pushed to the background.

Six o'clock Saturday morning, Bryan picked up Teresa at her house, then drove to the shelter. Michelle had just finished preparing toast and scrambled eggs for the boys and herself. Bryan and Teresa loaded the dishwasher and tidied the kitchen, while Michelle and the boys ate their breakfast.

"Mom, are you sure you have to go away?" Chuck pleaded. "I don't want you to leave us."

"Honey, I don't want to leave you, either, but it has to be done," Michelle replied as she hugged her son. "We can't go on living like this. I have to get better. Pastor Olson will take good care of you, and he promised to bring you to Great Falls every two weeks to see me. Just keep thinking about what we can do when I'm better. I'll be able to get a job and find a home of our own."

"I know, Mom." The young boy choked back his sobs, "but I want to stay with you. I don't want you to be sad anymore."

Michelle's eyes again became distant. Silently, she turned and went to her room. Within minutes she returned, carrying a small suitcase, which she sat in front of the door. She sank onto the sofa and buried her face in her hands. A cloud of gloom hung over the entire family as the boys went to their room to get their coats.

The ride to Great Falls was tense. Michelle stared out the window without saying a word the entire trip. The pain of her depression was more than she could bear, but love for her sons motivated her to keep going and seek professional help. The boys occasionally snapped at each other, while Teresa and Bryan tried to carry on light conversation.

Meanwhile, Bryan was wondering if he would make a good stand-in father. Teresa wondered if she would make a good wife. Richie and Chuck worried about their mother, while Michelle felt frozen and numb. Could she ever escape the depth of her depression?

When they finally arrived at the Great Falls hospital, Teresa helped Michelle complete the admission forms; then Michelle turned to say good-bye to her sons. She took both of them into her arms at the same time and sobbed.

"Maybe the boys would like to come and see the room where you will be staying for the next few weeks," a nurse's aide suggested. "We encourage family togetherness as much as possible. We'd like the boys to see your room and meet the people who will be important to you. If fact, we have an activity room where you can be together and enjoy each other's company for a couple of hours. It will make the transition much easier. We can order lunch trays from the cafeteria for them."

Chuck looked up at Bryan with pleading eyes. "Pastor, can we stay for just a little while?"

Bryan nodded his approval. "Of course you may," he assured them. "Teresa and I have some shopping to do, but we'll be back around two o'clock. Afterward we want to take you to the mall so you can pick out bedspreads and curtains for your new room. We'll even hit the boys' clothing department before we leave."

"Really?" Richie exclaimed. "You'd let us buy brand-new things?"

Pastor Olson bent over and looked both boys directly in the eyes. "A lot of people in Rocky Bluff are very concerned about you. To show their love, they took up a collection to help you get started in your new life."

"Wow, thanks," they chimed in unison.

As Teresa and Bryan left the hospital, the crisp spring air stung their cheeks. "I know Michelle feels as if this is the lowest day of her life," Teresa began as they walked across the parking lot, "but I'm excited for her. I see this as the start of a whole new life for her. She has so much potential."

"How true." Bryan took her hand. "I hope that we'll be able to help the boys reach *their* potential. They both have a long way to go, and I've never been a father before. It's easy to give advice to others, but it's entirely different when you're faced with the same situations."

"I guess you'll have to follow your own advice and pray, expect God to answer those prayers, and live one day at a time," Teresa chided.

Bryan wrapped his arm around her slender waist. "The first thing I want to do as soon as Michelle is out of the hospital and the family is reunited is to make you my wife. It's not fair to expect you to move into the parsonage before then when you'd be acquiring not only a husband but a ready-made family."

Teresa smiled defiantly at him. "Why not? I've been helping care for them while they've been at the shelter."

"You're one of a kind," Bryan replied as he pulled her closer to himself. "If you're sure, let's plan a wedding for the first weekend in June. We'll plan the biggest gala affair Rocky Bluff has seen in years."

"How about asking Pastor Rhodes to come back and perform the ceremony?" Teresa asked. "He has meant so much to me through the years."

"I'll contact him as soon as we get home," he said as he opened the door of the Jeep for Teresa. "Now, off to the jewelry store."

Early the next morning, Teresa rang the door to the parsonage. "I'm glad to see you," Bryan said as he opened the door. "On Sunday mornings I'm used to eating a quick bowl of cereal and hurrying to the church. Today I've got a couple of hungry boys to feed."

"That's why I came." Teresa took off her

coat and headed for the kitchen. "I'll fix their breakfast, and we'll be there before church starts. I know I won't have any trouble getting them to wear their new clothes."

"Teresa, you don't know how much I appreciate this," Bryan said as he took her in his arms. He raised her left hand to admire the quarter-karat diamond on her left hand. "That is the most beautiful ring I have ever seen, and you are the most beautiful woman I've ever known. Today is our big day. We can shout our love from the mountaintop. After church today our engagement will become public knowledge."

Just then, Richie entered the kitchen rubbing the sleep from his eyes. "What's for breakfast?" he mumbled.

"How about pancakes?" Teresa replied as she reached for the griddle in the cupboard next to the stove.

Richie's eyes brightened. "I love pancakes."

"Good. Go wake Chuck while I'm getting them ready," Teresa replied. "While you're at it, lay out the clothes you want to wear to church. Then as soon as you finish eating, you can take a quick shower."

Bryan grabbed his suit coat and tie, gave Teresa a quick kiss, and hurried out the door. While she was fixing the pancakes, she could hear the boys' excited voices from their bedrooms. She heard the crackle of cellophane as they hurriedly unwrapped their new clothes and laid them neatly on their beds. For the first time in their lives, they were going to wear brand-new, store-bought clothes.

An hour later Teresa and the two boys slipped quietly into the back pew of the Rocky Bluff Community Church. The boys' eyes became like saucers as they surveyed the stained-glass windows of the simple church and the beautiful altar. They had been inside a church only once before, at their grandfather's funeral.

As the pews filled up, the two boys scanned the congregation, trying to find people they knew from school. Chuck pointed to Valerie Snyder. Richie pointed toward the fifth-grade teacher. They both recognized Bob Harkness who ran the hardware store. They shuddered when they spotted the chief of police, Philip Mooney.

Just as the organ began to play, Nathan Brown walked in with his parents and took the pew two rows in front of them. The boys exchanged puzzled glances. The Browns were the first Afro-American family they had ever seen. They had expected them to not be very bright, but Nathan was the smartest kid in the sixth grade. The Frank boys had felt threatened by all the attention he had gotten at school, and they had vented their feelings by spray painting racial slurs on the Browns' garage. They had heard their father make derogatory remarks about people from other races, but now, to the boys' amazement, the people sitting around them greeted the Browns with genuine warmth. The Browns, the boys realized, were well respected by everyone but themselves.

During the service Chuck and Richie tried to do everything everyone else did. They studied the bulletin, but it made little sense to them. They decided to copy everything Nathan did. When Nathan stood, so did they; they bowed their heads when he did; and Teresa helped them find the hymns and the Scripture readings. They exchanged glances and grinned, glad to be part of the large, happy congregation.

After the sermon and the closing hymn, instead of walking to the back to greet the people, Pastor Olson motioned for the congregation to be seated. Everyone exchanged puzzled looks.

"Friends, I have two announcements to make concerning my personal life. First of all," he began slowly, trying to choose exactly the right words, "I am now the stand-in father for Chuck and Richie Frank while their mother is away receiving treatment. I hope you all will welcome them with open arms into our church family." The boys blushed as everyone gave them a round of applause.

Pastor Olson took a deep breath as his eyes settled on the mature, beautiful woman sitting beside the boys. "An even bigger change in my life will come about the first weekend in June." Every eye widened, and people leaned forward with interest. "Teresa Lennon has agreed to become my wife . . . and Pastor Rhodes has agreed to return to Rocky Bluff to perform the ceremony. You are all invited to the wedding."

A gasp spread through the sanctuary, followed by an even louder round of applause. Tears filled Teresa's eyes as people crowded around her with congratulations, wishing her God's continued blessings. Pastor Olson walked to the back of the church to greet a cheerful congregation that was filled with love and good wishes. The uncharted waters he was entering did not feel near as lonely now; after all, he realized, he and Teresa had their church's love and prayers to support them.

# CHAPTER 11

Dawn Harkness hurried up the sidewalk toward the Rocky Bluff Spouse Abuse Shelter. Today, instead of seeking support, she was bursting with excitement. She rang the doorbell and waited impatiently.

"Guess what?" she said as soon as Teresa opened the door. She stepped through the doorway, and without giving Teresa time to respond, she continued, "I've been accepted into summer school at Montana State University in Bozeman."

A broad smile spread across Teresa's face. Dawn's emotional roller-coaster rides had leveled out, and she was now ready to face life with dignity and purpose. Teresa patted the edge of the sofa. "Sit down and tell me all about it."

"Montana State has accepted my poor grades from Montana A&M and admitted me on academic probation," Dawn stated excitedly. "I'm sure if I stay away from the parties and work hard I can get my grade point up in a semester or two."

"I have all the confidence in the world that you can do it," Teresa replied. "You've come a long way this past year."

"Thanks to you," Dawn answered, unable to mask her love and respect for the woman beside her. "I'm really excited about going to summer school when the schedule is more relaxed. The timing is perfect. Jay and Angie will have had their baby by then, and Angie's mother will be here from Guam to help them. It will also be easier for Dad to hire help in the summer instead of later in the year. In fact, he already has someone in mind whom he'd like to give a chance at the job."

Teresa raised her eyebrows, her interest piqued. "And who's that?"

"Michelle Frank," Dawn replied. "I understand she's progressing better than expected in her treatment, and rumor has it she should be home by the time the boys are out of school for the summer."

Teresa smiled and nodded. "The rumors are true," she replied. "Her love for her sons has really motivated her to get well. I'm thrilled your dad is considering offering her a job when she comes home. That will speed recovery. She felt uncomfortable about having to live on welfare."

The pair then discussed the impact Bryan Olson had had on Michelle's sons. As soon as Bryan's name was mentioned, Dawn noticed the way Teresa glowed. Dawn smiled. "And how are the wedding plans coming?"

"All the details of the ceremony are falling into place," Teresa replied. "I've already ordered my dress, the flowers, and the invitations, and I've made arrangements with a photographer. I'm going to have Chuck and Richie serve as junior groomsmen. My sister is coming from Boise to be my matron of honor. She says she can't imagine me getting married and has to see it with her own eyes."

Dawn shook her head. "I don't understand why people are surprised when people get married later in life. It's a normal occurrence in Rocky Bluff. Grandma seems to have blazed the trail and demonstrated to the community that mature love is often the most satisfying and fulfilling love there is."

"It's certainly a lot different for me," Teresa agreed, then immediately changed the subject. "Dawn, I'm sorry I haven't had a chance to call you, but I was wondering if you would be willing to sit at the guest-book table at our wedding. You have such a sweet, welcoming charm about you. You're good at putting people at ease."

Dawn's eyes widened. "You actually want me to be a part of your wedding, after I've been such a pile of trouble for you?"

"Of course I do," Teresa persisted. Her tone became stern and loving at the same time. "And you have not been a pile of trouble. You've been one strong, brave woman to face your mistakes the way you did and turn your life around. I'm extremely proud of your accomplishments, and I'm sure your family is as well."

Dawn giggled. "Especially Grandma. She took me on as a personal prayer project and loved me through times when I was unlovable. I'm going to really miss her when I go to Bozeman."

After Dawn left the shelter, Teresa returned to her work with renewed vigor. There were so many discouraging moments in her line of work that she cherished the success stories.

She was hoping the Frank family would also become a success story. The boys had already painted over the epithets on many of the town garages. After school today, they were scheduled to repaint Angie and Jay's garage. Under Bryan's careful guidance they had learned to accept responsibility for their actions. Best of all, Nathan Brown was fast becoming one of their closest friends.

The boys had joined the Scouts just in time to be a part of a weekend campout and survival-skills training. Now they could talk about nothing else. The day of the campout was fast approaching.

"Boys, are you ready to go?" Bryan Olson shouted as he loaded their sleeping bags into the back of the Jeep.

"We'll be right there," Chuck shouted back. The boys grabbed their duffel bags and raced toward the car.

"I've never been on a campout before," Richie exclaimed as he slid into the backseat and threw his duffel bag behind the seat.

Bryan started the engine. "This is more than a Boy Scouts' campout. It's a weekend of wilderness survival. Every person growing up in Montana needs survival skills, and Scott Packwood is an expert in that area."

"I know survival skills are important," twelve-year-old Chuck replied with confidence. "I heard some kids at school talking about their father who got lost in the mountains while he was hunting and had to spend the night alone in a shelter he built himself."

Bryan turned the corner and headed toward the parking lot where the Scout troop was gathering. "I hope you boys learn a lot this weekend and have fun too."

"Oh, we will," Richie chimed in. "Nathan is going to be there, and he promised to share a tent with us."

When Bryan parked the car, the boys bounded out and raced toward the group of boys, their leaders, and several fathers. "I'm here," Richie shouted. "When are we going to leave?"

"We're all loaded," Scott Packwood said. "We were waiting for you to get here. Would you boys like to ride in my rig with Nathan?"

"Yeah!" they shouted. Grabbing their sleeping bags and duffel bags, they raced toward Scott Packwood's crew-cab pickup.

Bryan waited as the caravan of vehicles left the parking lot. *This will be a weekend the boys will remember for a long time.* He got back in his Jeep and sighed. This would also be a weekend he could devote entirely to Teresa and his congregation.

The caravan carrying Troop 95 wound up the narrow road to a clearing midway up the mountain. The boys laughed and cheered with each jolt of the vehicle. About fifty miles out of town, the troop reached a wide place in the road where they parked their vehicles. Each of the boys gathered their gear and began hiking up a narrow mountain path. They sang marching songs as they went along.

Although Chuck and Richie had spent most of their growing-up years in the woods, this trip was entirely different from what they had experienced in their cabin. Their father had not let them explore the surrounding terrain. Never before had they followed a path to see where it led or followed a creek around a bend.

When the troop arrived in a clearing, each group of boys began to select a site where they could pitch their tent. Nathan, Chuck, and Richie chose the site farthest to the north. Nearby there was a path that disappeared between the trees toward the summit of the mountain. The boys hurriedly pitched their tent, arranged their things, and gathered with the others in the center of the clearing.

Scoutmaster Packwood was just beginning to give his directions to the group. "Boys, it's getting late and will be dark soon, so we're going to fix basic hot dogs over an open flame for dinner tonight. I know you're all getting hungry after that long hike. Let's hurry and gather wood for our fire, and I'll show you ways to start a fire without matches."

The boys scattered and began picking up twigs. Some took out their pocketknives and cut off small branches. The three tent mates looked at each other. "Everyone else is getting wood nearby," Chuck exclaimed. "Let's get our wood farther down the path near our tent."

"We really don't need to go that far," Nathan protested.

"Sure we do," Chuck retorted. "We might find some wood that burns better than the picked-over stuff the others are getting."

Chuck pushed a branch aside as the three entered the narrow path. The ground was soft and mushy, and a few piles of snow remained in sheltered areas. The fresh breeze of springtime invited them on.

"Most of the wood out here will be too green to burn," Nathan noted as he pulled a lower limb toward him.

"Yeah, this stuff is wet," Richie replied, trying to sound knowledgeable.

Chuck was already several yards ahead of them. "Hey, there's a creek up here. I bet we can find some dry wood upstream."

The boys skipped from stone to stone in

the middle of the creek bed. "I'm sure glad Pastor Olson bought us these new sneakers," Chuck exclaimed, "otherwise I'd be sliding into the water."

Nathan looked up through the heavy overhang of pine tree branches. "It's starting to get dark. Don't you think we'd better get our wood and head back?"

The two brothers looked up and shrugged their shoulders. "It's still light," Richie replied. "It's just getting a little cloudy."

Chuck was well ahead of the others and had just turned another bend in the creek. "Nathan, Richie, come see. . . . Here's a beaver dam."

Nathan and Richie hurried around the bend to where Chuck was standing beside a pile of dry sticks in the middle of the creek. Suddenly, Richie lurched sideways, as his foot slipped on a rock. The evening quiet was broken by a large splash followed by a screech of pain.

"Richie, are you okay?" Nathan exclaimed as he knelt over his friend.

Richie remained motionless. He moaned, while his brother raced toward him. "Come on, Richie. Get up. You're going to get soaked lying there," Chuck cried.

Richie moaned again. "I can't. My leg hurts."

"Here, we'll help." Nathan and Chuck each took hold of the injured boy and dragged him out of the stream to a grassy knoll.

"I'll go back and get help," Nathan said as Richie's moaning turned to sobs.

"But it's starting to get dark," Chuck protested. "Did you bring a flashlight?"

"Mine's in my duffel bag back at the campsite," Nathan gasped.

"So's mine," Chuck said as he glanced down at his younger brother. "Look, he's shaking. He's all wet and getting cold. I'm scared. What are we going to do?"

"I guess we're going to have to stay here until it's light again," Nathan replied as he surveyed the sky. "See, there's only a little sliver of a moon tonight. And it's so cloudy there probably won't be any stars."

"My friend's dad who got lost while he was hunting built an overnight shelter for himself," Chuck said as he surveyed the nearby terrain.

Nathan looked around, then pointed to a cluster of trees. "See those two trees with the bush between them? They look like they could make a little cave. Maybe we could get dead branches to build a roof."

Chuck nodded in agreement. "We better work fast while we still have a little light.

Let's drag Richie over there, out of the wind."

The two boys pulled Richie under the bush, while he sobbed with pain. They made a pillow for his head from a pile of dry leaves. Then Nathan and Chuck scurried deeper into the woods and grabbed up armloads of sticks.

They raced back to their makeshift shelter and placed the sticks on the bush, making a three-foot-wide overhang. They worked until the sky was completely dark, and they could no longer see their way through the trees.

Nathan and Chuck snuggled into the shelter beside Richie. The hoots of night owls echoed through the trees, mingling with distant coyotes' howls. Richie's moans became softer.

"I hope Richie will be all right," Chuck said between chattering teeth. "I'm scared."

"So am I," Nathan replied as he snuggled even closer to the brothers.

"I want my mommy," Richie sobbed. "Why did she have to go away?"

"Mom's in the hospital, and they're making her better," Chuck replied with tears in his eyes. "We had a lot of fun with her last week when Pastor Olson and Teresa took us to see her. I've never seen her so happy.

She's going to be home soon."

Richie continued to sob. "But I want my mommy, *now!*"

Chuck began to cry along with his brother. All the pent-up anguish of years of physical and emotional abuse poured out. Richie's physical pain was intensified by his fear and emotional pain. The brothers held each other and sobbed. After awhile their sobs turned to hiccups, and they began to talk quietly about the fear they had of their father, their loneliness, and their feelings of being misunderstood. They talked about their remorse for spray painting racial graffiti, about their love for their mother, about the day she would be out of the hospital and they could be a family again.

Outside their makeshift shelter, snow began to fall, and the temperature dropped. The ground froze. The boys' footprints in the soggy path and along the creek bed were now hidden under the snow.

Nathan snuggled close and listened to the brothers talk. He thought about his own family . . . his mother and father in Rocky Bluff . . . his grandparents, aunts, uncles, and cousins in South Carolina. *What would they do if they were here?* he pondered, trying to calm his panic. He tried to picture each of them sitting in the shelter with them; then he knew what they would have done. They would have prayed.

"Dear God," Nathan whispered, "I never paid much attention during the times Mama made me go to Sunday school and church, and I'm not sure how to pray, but please help us. Help somebody find us."

Chuck choked back a sob and turned to his friend. "Do you actually believe in God? Do you think He'll answer our prayers?"

"Yeah, I guess so," Nathan replied. "Whenever anything happens in our family, everyone prays, and things seem to work out. I guess there's nothing else we can do so we might as well pray."

"But I don't know how to pray," Chuck admitted cautiously. "Until we moved into the parsonage, I never heard anyone pray before. Praying is Pastor Olson's job. He uses all kinds of big fancy words. I don't know how to talk like that."

"Mama just talks to God like she talks to the rest of the family. She begins by saying, 'Dear Heavenly Father,' and she closes by saying, 'In Jesus' name. Amen.' "

Chuck took a deep breath to regain his composure. "That sounds easy enough. Let's give it a try."

Nathan looked at the brothers. Richie's

eyes were closed, and he was breathing heavily, still moaning. "Okay," he said. "I guess we're supposed to bow our heads and fold our hands."

Richie appeared to have slipped into a painful sleep, but the two other boys bowed their heads and closed their eyes. Nathan took a deep breath. "Dear Heavenly Father, I don't know how to pray, but please help us. Richie is hurt real bad, and we don't know how to get him out of here. Help them find us. Don't let anything bad happen to Richie. Don't let us freeze to death. In Jesus' name. Amen."

Chuck opened his eyes, leaned closer to his brother, trying to see his face, then turned back to Nathan. "My friend told me that when his dad was lost in the woods he had to force himself to stay awake. He said that if he went to sleep he would have never woken up again."

"Yeah, I heard that happens when a person gets too cold and goes to sleep," Nathan replied. "Maybe we'd better try to keep Richie awake. There's no way anyone can find us until daylight." He took a deep breath. "Guess it's going to be a pretty long night."

# CHAPTER 12

Scott Packwood surveyed the scout troop crowded around the fire, each boy holding a stick with a hot dog roasting on the end. Darkness was beginning to settle over the mountain, and Scott had the uneasy feeling that something was wrong. He counted bodies. He counted again. His heart pounded as he realized three boys were missing. He began to mentally run down the list of boys. *Where were the Frank boys and Nathan Brown?*

"Hey, guys. Listen up," Scoutmaster Packwood shouted. "Has anyone seen Chuck, Richie, and Nathan?"

The boys exchanged puzzled glances. Everyone shook their head.

"I haven't seen them since they pitched their tent next to ours," a freckle-faced boy replied as he pulled his hot dog away from the flame.

"Which one is their tent?" Scott asked.

"The dark blue one at the far end," the boy replied.

The scoutmaster and Ed Running Tail, one of the fathers, took their flashlights to the distant tent. Scott shone his flashlight inside. "It looks like all their stuff is here," he said grimly, "so if they've wandered away, they don't have any survival gear with them."

Ed flashed his beam on the surrounding ground. As an avid deer hunter he had become an expert at spotting minor disturbances of ground cover. He walked toward the path heading into the trees. He paused. "Scott, come here."

Scott hurried to Ed's side. "Look at this," Ed exclaimed. "We have footprints and broken lower branches leading into the woods this direction. Those boys must have gone exploring as soon as they got here."

Scott sucked in a breath, while adrenaline surged through his body. "Let's have the other chaperons get the boys singing around the campfire. You and I will go look for them."

He hurried back to the campfire, explained the situation to the other leaders, and asked them to take responsibility for the troop while he and Ed Running Tail searched for the missing boys. He then followed Ed down the narrow path.

Ed kept the beam of his flashlight focused on the ground in front of him as they walked. When they came to the creek, they leaped across and resumed searching the ground for footprints. After walking scarcely five feet more, Ed stopped.

"I've lost the footprints," Ed sighed. "There's just no way we can pick up their trail in the dark."

Scott sighed and shook his head. "Let's go back to camp. I brought a cellular phone so we can call for help."

Arriving at the campsite, Scott raced toward his tent. He took out his duffel bag, rummaged through its contents, and found his cellular phone. He hurriedly pressed the numbers 9-1-1. The scoutmaster explained the details to the police dispatcher. As he broke the connection with the Rocky Bluff Police Department, a sense of helplessness overwhelmed him. All he could do was wait for daylight.

He let the boys sing songs and tell ghost stories far into the night. When their eyes became heavy at last, he urged the boys to retire to their tents. While one by one the whispering in the tents subsided, the adults gathered around the fire and waited.

"I'm really scared about those kids," Scott

said as he paced back and forth in front of the flames. "Nathan Brown just moved here from South Carolina. . . . He wouldn't have any survival skills. Although the Frank brothers spent most of their lives in a cabin in the woods, they were never allowed very far from their father's eyes. I was shocked at how ignorant they were about the basics of outdoor life."

As the men planned their strategy for an early morning search party, a light snow began to fall. Little by little the flakes became larger and closer together. The ground was soon glistening with a half inch of snow.

"We're going to have a hard time finding them with their tracks covered by the snow," Ed Running Tail noted, "and with the snow their chances of suffering hypothermia increases."

Scott continued pacing around the fire. "I'll call my wife and have her make arrangements for someone to come and get the other boys first thing in the morning. We'll keep the food here to help feed the search parties. Outside of that, there's nothing we can do until morning. Except pray." The flames reflected off Scott's neon orange hunting jacket as he squatted beside the fire and bowed his head. "Let's take a few minutes of silence and each pray for the boys' safety."

As soon as the Rocky Bluff police dispatcher received Scott Packwood's emergency call, the town of Rocky Bluff sprang into action. The volunteer search and rescue team members began to assemble. The hospital was notified, and an EMT crew along with an off-duty nurse responded. A local pilot volunteered to fly aerial reconnaissance. The K-9 Academy was notified, and three trained tracking dogs and their handlers were dispatched from Great Falls. The police department became the hub of activity.

Police Chief Philip Mooney called Bryan Olson. Pastor Olson was working late in his study when the phone rang, and the police chief quickly told him the bad news. "We're organizing search and rescue teams. The first will be heading out to the mountain in about an hour. Do you think the women of the church could prepare meals for them?"

Bryan took a deep breath, trying to calm the panic that raced through him. "I'll call the president of our women's group, Rebecca Hatfield. Although it's late, I'm sure she and her husband will do anything they can to help. Her husband is experienced at handling crises."

"The Browns have already been contacted, and they're on their way to the campsite. What should we do about notifying the Frank boys' mother?"

"It's too late to get in touch with her tonight," Bryan replied. "Hopefully, by morning we'll have some good news for her. I'd hate to worry her if we don't have to, especially about something she's helpless to do anything about. I'm afraid it could send her back into depression. She's been doing so well lately."

Bryan and Philip finished coordinating their plans and ended their conversation. Bryan hurriedly found the Hatfields' telephone number.

Although she was awakened from a sound sleep, Rebecca readily agreed to plan food and hot drinks for the search and rescue team. She knew that this night, like the night several years before when her neighbors' house had burned, she would have no sleep.

Bryan then dialed Teresa's number. "Hello," a sleepy voice greeted him.

"Hello, Teresa. It's me," he responded. "I hate to bother you so late at night, but the boys and Nathan Brown wandered away from their troop and are lost in the woods.

A search and rescue operation is being organized. I'm going to be gathering some gear and heading for the mountain in a few minutes. Do you want to come along?"

"Of course I want to go!" Teresa bolted upright in bed. "I'll make a thermos of coffee and gather some extra blankets."

"Great," Bryan replied. "I called the Hatfields, and they're going to be preparing food and drinks for the search and rescue personnel. I think I've done as much as I can from here. I'll be over to get you in fifteen minutes."

Teresa ran a comb through her tousled hair and pulled on a pair of insulated underwear and sweats. This was definitely not a time to worry about fashion. She filled her coffee percolator and took her thermos from the top cupboard. While the coffee was perking, she went to the hall closet and took out three extra blankets and a sleeping bag. She took her parka, boots, and gloves and laid them on a chair by the door. By the time the coffee was done, the doorbell rang.

Bryan stuck his head in the door. "Teresa, are you about ready?" he shouted.

"Come on in," she called back. "I'm in the kitchen."

Bryan gave Teresa a quick kiss on the cheek as she finished pouring the coffee into the thermos. "I hope you dressed warmly. They say snow is predicted for above five thousand feet. The campsite is halfway up the mountain."

"I have my long johns on," she assured him. She stood on tiptoe to kiss the worried lines that creased his face. "They're in God's hands," she reminded him softly.

"I know." He took a deep breath and squared his shoulders. "I brought a change of clothes for the boys. I'm glad we got them insulated underwear and sweatshirts in Great Falls. I'm feeling sick about what they're wearing now. I'd assumed they would have dressed warmly, but judging by what I found in their rooms they dressed for the weather in Rocky Bluff, not in the mountains. Even their hiking boots were still in their rooms. I could kick myself for not checking them over before they left." He grimaced. "Some stand-in father I am."

Teresa screwed on the lid of the thermos, then took Bryan's hand. "You can't blame yourself. You're just not used to being a father. Besides, no one predicted the weather would change this abruptly."

"Maybe the weatherman didn't predict this, but common sense from living in Montana would," Bryan replied with disgust in his voice. "It's always a lot colder in the mountains. That's one of the survival skills I wanted them to learn this weekend."

*I'm sure they've learned it now, but I hope they haven't suffered too much in the meantime,* Teresa thought as she put on her coat and boots.

Soon, Teresa and Bryan were bouncing along on the narrow road up the mountain toward the campsite. Several sets of vehicle lights could be spotted on the usually desolate road. Five miles from the turn-off it began to snow. The higher they climbed, the heavier the snow fell. "It's times like this I'm glad I have a four-wheel drive," Bryan said absently, his mind on the missing boys.

As they neared the campsite, they saw a string of vehicles along the roadside. Bryan pulled the Jeep to a stop behind the last parked car, and Teresa reached for the thermos and a bag of Styrofoam cups from the backseat. Together they hiked the last quarter mile to where the others were gathered. An ambulance, two EMTs, and a nurse were already there, along with several volunteers waiting for daybreak.

Through the long night the boys huddled together in their makeshift shelter. Nathan and Chuck had to keep shaking Richie to make sure he stayed awake. Toward dawn it quit snowing, and the temperature began to drop. "I can't feel my toes," Chuck whispered to Nathan. "You don't think they'll drop off, do you?"

Nathan's eyes widened. "I don't think so, but I don't know. I've never been this cold in my life."

"I wish I'd worn my old hiking boots instead of the new sneakers that Teresa and Pastor Olson bought for me," Chuck moaned.

"Yeah, that was pretty dumb," Nathan replied.

"I don't think God heard us when we prayed. Maybe He's mad at us because of all the bad stuff Richie and I did." Chuck gulped back tears. "What if we freeze to death? Will they just dig a hole and put us in the ground, or will they use a casket?"

"Chuck, quit talking that way," Nathan scolded. "They're going to find us when it gets light. I know they will. My mama always tells me that God loves me even more than she does and that He'll always forgive me if I do something bad, so long as I'm sorry. You and Richie aren't the same as you used to be. God knows you're sorry for what you did." He lifted his chin and said firmly, "He's going to answer our prayer. Just you wait."

"But what if He doesn't? What if no one ever finds us, not until it's too late and we've all frozen to death?"

"As soon as it starts to get light, I'll walk back to camp myself," Nathan stated bravely.

"Do you know how to get back?"

Nathan bit his lip. "I can't remember for sure, and everything will look different when it's covered with snow," he admitted. "While we were running along the creek bank, we passed some other paths. I won't know which one leads back to camp."

"Maybe we'd better stay together." Chuck clung tighter to both his friend and his brother. "I'd be scared without you."

"Do you think anyone has missed us by now?" Nathan's voice wobbled. For all his brave words earlier, he too was scared. "Maybe they won't miss us until it's time to go back home. That won't be until tomorrow."

As a pink glow appeared in the east, Nathan crawled outside their shelter and looked around. Within minutes he was back. "It looks so different covered with snow." He ducked back into the shelter. "There's a clearing across the creek. I'm going to walk over there and write the letters H-E-L-P. Maybe an airplane will fly over and see it. They did that last week on a TV show I saw."

Chuck muffled a sob. "I'd help you, but I can't stand up. My feet hurt too much."

"Just stay here with Richie," Nathan replied. "I can do it myself." He slipped outside and trudged across the creek, then walked down the creek bank until he was at the far left of the clearing. He jumped onto the bank and dragged his feet through the snow until the four letters were formed. A sense of exhilaration filled him as he leaped back across the creek. At least he had done something, something that might help them be found.

"All we can do now is sit back and hope someone sees our signal." Nathan looked down at Richie. The injured boy had a distant, glazed look in his eyes.

"I'm thirsty," he whimpered.

"Should we give him some snow to eat?" Chuck asked.

Nathan shook his head. "I read in a book that people freeze to death faster if they eat snow. I'll go down to the creek and try to get some water. It'll be pretty cold, but at least it'll be warmer than snow. I'll only be able to bring back what I can carry in my bare hands, though."

Richie moved his head from side to side. "Please . . . water."

About fifty men and women had gathered at the scouts' campsite by six o'clock that morning. The Hatfields were there with food, hot chocolate, and coffee. Dawn Harkness was there with three of her friends. Three tracking dogs were ready. The EMTs and the nurse had all the equipment necessary to treat hypothermia. The aircraft had been gassed and was ready to roll. The volunteers were divided into groups of four, each carrying a handheld radio.

When the searchers dispersed, Dawn Harkness turned to one of her friends. "If I were a kid and had just pitched my tent, I'd want to see where this path behind my tent led."

"That's where Ed Running Tail said he saw some footprints before it started to snow," one of her partners agreed, "but there's no guarantee it was their footprints and not someone else's. But without any other clues it's worth a try."

Dawn led her group down the path. Wet branches swatted them in the face as they went. When they got to the creek, Dawn stopped. "Okay, if you were a ten-year-old boy, which way would you go?" she asked the group.

"I've always been fascinated with rivers," one of her companions replied. "I'd have followed the creek."

"Upstream or downstream?" Dawn asked.

"Upstream," he replied. "The challenge is always to climb a mountain, not walk down a mountain."

The snow became deeper, and the pace of the search party slowed. The buzz of a single-engine plane echoed overhead. They watched as the plane seemed to be making smaller and smaller circles ahead of them.

Suddenly, the handheld radio in Dawn's hand squawked. "Attention all searchers. The pilot has spotted what looks like the letters H-E-L-P trampled in the snow in a clearing near the creek, northwest of the campsite. Whoever's in that area, would you please check it out?"

Dawn pushed the speak button. "This is Dawn Harkness. We're heading up the creek bank in that direction."

"Let us know as soon as you find them," a deep voice replied. "Don't try to bring them out yourself. Take careful note of their condition, and the nurse will help us decide what to do."

The foursome trudged on up the creek

bank for another hundred yards. As they turned a bend in the creek, one of them shouted, "There's the clearing with the letters! They have to be close by."

"Chuck! . . . Richie! . . . Nathan! . . . Can you hear me?" Dawn shouted.

Nathan ran out of the shelter, and Chuck crawled as close to the opening as he could without standing. "We're here! We're here!" the boys shouted.

The foursome raced toward the makeshift shelter. Nathan clung to the first person who got to them. "You found us. You found us," he cried.

Dawn got down on her hands and knees and crawled into their shelter. She hugged Chuck who immediately burst into tears. "How are you boys doing?" she asked.

"Richie's hurt real bad," Chuck cried. "He can't walk, and he looks really funny. My feet used to hurt, but now I don't feel them at all. I can't walk on them. How are we going to get out of here?"

"There's all kinds of help at the campsite. I have a radio in my jacket. I'll let them know we've found you, and that you and Richie can't walk out."

Sounds of cheers echoed throughout the mountainside as word spread that the boys had been found alive. Bryan's eyes met Teresa's for a long moment. "Thank You, God," he whispered. Within minutes the nurse, EMTs, three stretchers, food, drinks, blankets, and scores of searchers descended on the boys' makeshift shelter.

As the nurse examined the boys, Pastor Olson led the others in a prayer of thanksgiving for caring for the boys through the long, cold night. He asked God that their injuries would heal quickly. Chuck listened, his eyes shining, and when Bryan said "amen," the boy pulled on his jacket sleeve.

"Pastor Olson," he cried, "Nathan and I prayed that somebody would find us. And God heard us. He really did." For the first time in their lives, he and his brother had experienced the power of prayer.

# CHAPTER 13

The ambulance bearing the boys raced down the mountain. The nurse had placed a temporary splint on Richie's leg and had wrapped all three boys in several blankets.

Bryan Olson rode in the front seat of the ambulance and nervously looked over his shoulder as the nurse and EMT treated the boys. *This is all my fault. I should have checked to see what the boys were wearing before they left,* he chastised himself. *I should have warned them not to wander off by themselves. Their mother has enough to worry about just getting herself stabilized. She doesn't need this extra worry. And here I promised her that her boys would be well cared for.*

When the boys arrived at the hospital, the medical team immediately set to work. Nathan was evaluated, then released into the arms of his relieved parents. Chuck was admitted for hypothermia and frostbite. Richie was immediately whisked into X-ray.

Bryan paced back and forth, waiting for word on the boys' condition. Would Chuck lose any of his toes, or possibly both his feet, because of frostbite? How serious was Richie's injury? The questions haunted him, intruding on his prayer. *I know they're in Your hands, Lord. I just feel so guilty for not taking better care of them. Forgive me, Father. Please don't punish them for my mistakes.*

After reading the X-rays and consulting with other staff members, Dr. Brewer approached Pastor Olson. "Who is legally responsible for the boys at this time?"

Bryan shrugged his shoulders and sighed. "I'm responsible for them up to a point. I can approve all routine medical treatment. If there's anything serious, I think their mother needs to be contacted in the Great Falls hospital."

"It's serious," Dr. Brewer replied grimly. "I don't know yet if we'll be able to treat Chuck here in this hospital. It depends on how the circulation returns to his feet. If we have to amputate the little toe, I would be able to do it here. But if he requires more extensive surgery, I'd rather have it done in Great Falls." The doctor hesitated and took a deep breath. "Richie is a different matter."

A deep furrow creased the pastor's forehead. "How bad are his injuries?"

"They need specialized attention," the doctor replied. "Besides suffering from hypothermia and frostbite, he has a compound fracture, and the bone is nearly through the skin. It will take an orthopedic surgeon to set the leg properly. I'd suggest we medevac him to the Great Falls hospital right away."

"If we do that, they might as well take Chuck along and have him treated there as well," Bryan said. "I'll drive to Great Falls and stay with their mother. She's doing well and is scheduled to be released sometime next week."

Dr. Brewer stared out the window, lost in thought. "I'll call and talk to her doctor. I'll have him tell her the condition of her sons and that they will be arriving at the hospital within three hours. That way they'll be able to monitor her anxiety level until they arrive."

Pastor Olson extended his hand. "Thank you, Dr. Brewer. I appreciate all you're doing to help the boys."

As Dr. Brewer turned toward the doctors' lounge, Teresa entered the waiting room. She gave Bryan a hurried embrace. "How are they doing?"

"Richie is going to need surgery to set his leg. Dr. Brewer felt it would be better if it were done in Great Falls. They don't know yet if they'll have to amputate part of Chuck's feet or not, so both boys are going to be medevacked to Great Falls." He studied his fiancée's mud-splattered face. "As soon as I change clothes, I'm going to be leaving for Great Falls. Would you come with me?"

"I wouldn't let you leave me behind," she replied. "I'm sorry it took me so long to get here. After the ambulance left, there were all kinds of traffic problems on the mountain. A bunch of cars got stuck in the snow and mud. Everyone had to take turns pushing them out."

"Did you have any trouble driving the Jeep?"

"It was different," Teresa admitted. "I'd never driven a four-wheel drive before, but I made it."

Bryan wrapped his arm around her waist as they headed for the door. "Better get used to it. It will soon be half yours."

Although neither one had had much sleep that night, within an hour both Bryan and Teresa had showered, changed clothes, and were on their way to Great Falls. "I'm going to have to drive back late tonight so I can get a few hours of sleep before Sunday morning services." Bryan turned onto the main highway outside of Rocky Bluff. "Would you like to come back with me, or would you rather stay in a motel in Great Falls?"

"I'd like to stay there until everyone is released from the hospital. Michelle is going to need all the support she can get," Teresa replied as she leaned her head against the back of the seat. She let her eyes fall shut.

The rolling wheat fields flew by as Bryan prayed silently for Michelle and her sons. Now and then he glanced at Teresa and smiled, glad that she could get some sleep. She awakened just as they merged with the traffic on Tenth Avenue South. "Are we here already?"

"Sure are."

"I feel a lot better after having slept. But I should have taken the wheel part of the way so you could sleep too." Teresa reached for Bryan's hand. "You must be exhausted."

"I'll be all right. I'm just anxious to get there."

When the pair arrived at the hospital, they went directly to Michelle's floor. The nurse at the station there told them that Richie was in surgery and Michelle was waiting with Chuck in his room on the third floor. Bryan and Teresa hurried back to the elevator, worried about Michelle's anxiety level. Having both sons in the hospital at the same time would be a hard load for any mother, but particularly hard for one who was only just recovering from a major depression. They were both prepared to deal with anything from hysterics to apathetic withdrawal, and outside Chuck's room they each took a deep breath and said a quick prayer for strength and wisdom.

When they had slipped into the room, though, their eyes widened with amazement. Michelle was sitting beside her sleeping son's bed, dressed in an attractive, teal-colored dress. Her hair was styled, and she was wearing makeup she had never worn before. Her face was grave but composed.

Teresa hurried to her side and embraced her. "I'm so sorry this happened," she said. "How are you doing?"

"I'm doing fine." Michelle smiled. "I'm scheduled to be released on Thursday."

Bryan stepped forward and shook Michelle's hand. "How are the boys doing?"

"Richie has been in surgery about an hour," she replied. "The doctors are very optimistic about his recovery. They said his biggest problem probably would be learning how to walk on crutches." Michelle looked over at her older son sleeping beside her. "They're keeping a close eye on Chuck. It appears that the circulation is returning to his feet except for the small toe on the left foot. I hope they don't have to amputate, but I feel he'll be lucky if that's the worst that happens."

Bryan looked seriously into the mother's hazel eyes. He sucked in a breath. "Michelle, I feel terrible about this. I should have noticed what kind of footwear the boys had on. I just assumed they would wear their old hiking boots instead of their new athletic shoes. I guess I wasn't cut out to be a stand-in father." He looked down at Chuck's sleeping face. "I'm so sorry. I wish there was something else I could say."

"There's no way you could have imagined this would happen," Michelle replied. "Before he went to sleep, Chuck was blaming himself for Richie's broken leg. He doesn't even mention his own pain. He claimed it was all his idea to go exploring when they were supposed to be gathering wood." She shook her head. "I'm the one who is to blame."

A puzzled look spread across Teresa's face.

"How can you say that? You weren't even there."

"If I had been a better parent, I'd have stood up to their father long ago. If he would have let the boys have some breathing room, they wouldn't have been so tempted to follow the first unknown path they saw." Her voice trembled. "I'm their mother. My first job is to take care of them, to do what's best for them. I got my priorities all mixed up . . . and I failed them." Her eyes filled with tears.

An understanding smile spread across Bryan's face. "I think I understand for the first time a little of what it means to be a parent. What an enormous responsibility." He squared his shoulders, then reached a hand out to Michelle. "None of us is perfect, Michelle, not you, not me. We all make mistakes, even when we have the best intentions. But we have a loving Father Who forgives all our sins and shortcomings. And our children are in His hands. He's the only One Who can truly keep them safe."

He squeezed Michelle's hand. "A lot of prayers went up last night for the boys' safety. God answered those prayers and protected them." The pastor's smile broadened. "What amazes me is that without any survival skills training, they instinctively figured out how to build an ingenious shelter to protect themselves from the elements."

Michelle's eyes became distant. "I've always believed we have guardian angels looking after us," she said softly. Then she smiled. "It must take an entire legion of angels to take care of my two."

There was a rustle of movement outside the door, and a large man in surgical green stepped into the room. "Mrs. Frank?" the doctor queried. He looked back and forth between the two women.

Michelle stepped forward. "I'm Michelle Frank. How's my son?"

"Richie has a mighty nasty break and we had to insert a pin, but I think it will heal without any permanent damage. I'll send his records back to Dr. Brewer in Rocky Bluff so he can monitor its healing. Richie's a very lucky young man." The doctor smiled.

"Thank you, Doctor," Michelle said. "Everyone here has been so good to us. When can I see my son?"

"He's in the recovery room now. The orderlies will bring him up as soon as he comes out of the anesthesia. He should be able to go home Monday. In fact, if your other son continues to improve, he'll also be on his way home at the same time."

The doctor excused himself, and Michelle gazed at the empty bed in the room. "In a few minutes, I'll have both my sons under the same roof as me for the first time in six weeks," she said. "I've been praying for this day. But," she added dryly, "this wasn't quite how I had imagined it."

Bryan put his hand on her shoulder. "After Thursday you'll all be under the same roof in Rocky Bluff."

Just then Chuck stirred in his bed and opened his eyes. "Mom, Pastor, Teresa," he exclaimed. "You're all here. Where's Richie?"

"They just finished surgery on his leg, and he's going to be in this other bed in a few minutes," Michelle replied. "How are you feeling?"

Chuck grinned. "I can wiggle all my toes. See?" He pulled back the sheet and wiggled his toes to prove his point. Michelle couldn't see much movement through the bandages, but Chuck's declaration was enough to give her hope.

A few minutes later, Richie was wheeled into the room with his leg in a cast, suspended from a frame over the bed. Chuck raised his bed as his brother came into the room. "Hi. I bet I can finally run faster than you can."

Through sleepy eyes, Richie's face broke into a broad grin. He looked around at the smiling faces. "Hi, everyone. It's nice and warm in here." He closed his eyes and drifted into a peaceful sleep.

Teresa turned to Michelle. "I plan to stay here in Great Falls and help you until the boys are ready to go home, but I need to check into a motel for the night. Bryan has to get back to Rocky Bluff tonight so he can get ready for Sunday's services. I'll be back later."

Michelle turned to Pastor Olson. "I appreciate all you've done for me and the boys. I don't think I'll ever be able to repay you."

Pastor Olson gave the answer he gave to everyone who told him that they didn't know how to repay him. "Don't repay me. But when you're able, repay the debt to someone else who needs help."

"Thanks," Michelle murmured. "Don't worry. When I get back to Rocky Bluff, I'm going to be first on every volunteer list in town."

"Good," Pastor Olson said as he picked up his jacket to leave. "I'll be back Monday morning to get Teresa and the boys. Meanwhile, I'm going to be looking for a place for you and your family to stay. Bob Harkness said that you can start work as soon as you move back and are settled in Rocky Bluff. With planting season approaching, he says his business is beginning to pick up. He could use you as soon as possible."

After the Sunday service, Pastor Olson told his congregation that the Frank boys and their mother would be released from the hospital this week. "There is a box in the back of the church if anyone would like to contribute to help them set up a household again. They will also be looking for a place to rent," he explained. "Please talk to me if you have any suggestions."

Bob Harkness and his mother held back until everyone had shaken hands with the pastor. Seeing Edith in her wheelchair, Bryan approached them. "Good morning, Edith. I'm glad you could make it out today."

"I hate missing church, but it's getting harder and harder for me to leave the house," she replied. "Being here always rejuvenates me." Edith paused for a moment and moistened her lips. "You said that Michelle Frank and her boys are looking for a place to stay?"

"Yes," Pastor Olson replied. "Do you have any suggestions?"

"I'd be willing to let them live in my house free of charge until they get on their feet. All they would have to do is pay the utilities. We can work out a rent schedule later. It's obvious I'll never be able to live alone again, so someone should make good use of the hard work that Roy Dutton put into building that house. I had many happy years there with Roy, and I hope they'll enjoy it as much as I did."

"Edith, I can imagine how difficult this decision must be for you to make. You're cutting all ties to your old home." Bryan took her hand.

A tear glistened in Edith's eyes. "I've always tried to look forward with hope and never look back with regret. I have a comfortable life with Bob and his family. Lately, my mind has been dwelling on the past — my autumn love with Roy Dutton, and before that, the good life I had with George Harkness. I have much to be grateful for. I want to share what I can with others."

Pastor Olson looked at Bob who was nodding his head in agreement. "Letting the Franks use the house is the most unselfish act I have ever known," Bryan responded. "I'll be going to Great Falls tomorrow to bring the boys home. I'm sure Michelle will be thrilled to know she has a home waiting for her."

"I'm glad to still be useful," Edith replied. "I wanted to be out in the woods looking for them, but I have to accept my limitations."

Pastor Olson watched Bob push his mother's wheelchair out of the church. *Rocky Bluff is full of good people,* he thought, *but few have the strength of character of Edith Dutton.*

On Monday morning when Pastor Olson walked into the Frank boys' hospital room, he found them up and dressed. Richie was sitting in a wheelchair with a set of crutches beside him. Michelle and Teresa looked on lovingly.

"Hi, guys," Bryan greeted. "Are you ready to go home?"

"You bet," Richie replied. "Will they be having another campout? I wish I hadn't missed this one."

Bryan exchanged grins with Michelle and Teresa, then turned back to the boys. "They're planning to reschedule one sometime before school is out."

"One thing's for sure," Richie replied with a laugh. "I won't be able to wander away if

I'm on crutches."

Bryan turned his attention to Michelle. "I found a furnished house for you and the boys when you come home Thursday. Until you get settled, all you'll have to pay is the utilities."

Michelle's eyes widened with amazement. "Who would do that for us?" she gasped.

"Edith Dutton," Bryan replied. "She knows she will never be strong enough to live alone again. She hopes that the three of you will be as happy there as she and Roy were."

"She's amazing. I've heard she's done more for Rocky Bluff than anyone else," Michelle replied.

Michelle hugged the boys good-bye, knowing that in three days they would be a family once more. The six weeks of rest and rehabilitation on the psychiatric floor of the Great Falls hospital had restored her zest for life.

The nursing staff helped the Frank boys to Pastor Olson's Jeep, and they left for Rocky Bluff. They had a few more nights to sleep at the parsonage until their mother returned home.

That night after the boys were settled in their beds, Bryan and Teresa relaxed in the living room. This was the first time they had been alone together in over a week. "Now that the Franks's problems are beginning to smooth out, we should spend some time planning for our future," Bryan said as he slid an arm around her shoulders.

"Our wedding plans are coming along," Teresa replied softly. "I mailed the invitations over a week ago. It doesn't seem possible that in less than three weeks I'll be Mrs. Bryan Olson."

"With all the weddings we have both participated in, wedding details are the least of my concern," Bryan said as he pulled his fiancée against his chest. "We have moving plans to make . . . and we haven't even talked about a honeymoon."

"Why don't we take a honeymoon and not worry about moving until we get back," Teresa replied. "I think we both could use a long vacation."

"So where do you want to go on a honeymoon? It's got to be farther away than Billings." Bryan grinned.

"I've always had a secret desire to go to the Cayman Islands." Teresa looked rueful. "But I'm realistic enough not to even consider it."

"And why not? It never hurts to dream. I'm going to check into the Cayman Islands before we come up with alternate plans B or C. I've been saving for a rainy day for a long time, but the good Lord has protected me, and I haven't had too many rainy days." Bryan pulled her closer, and their lips melted onto each other's.

"Any place alone with you would be a honeymoon," Teresa whispered.

"I just hope we won't have any more crises in Rocky Bluff before or during our honeymoon. I don't want you to start your life as a pastor's wife dealing with someone else's problems."

"Bryan, please don't underestimate me," Teresa begged. "I love you, but I've also dedicated my life to helping the people of Rocky Bluff. We will walk this path together, and that's all I want. Never having any problems, that would be boring. But sharing the problems as they come, knowing that we're together . . ." She looked into his eyes. "You never need apologize to me again for the responsibilities that come with being a pastor's wife. God has work He wants me to do in this town. And I want to do it . . . with you by my side."

# CHAPTER 14

Jay Harkness and Rebecca Hatfield sat in the waiting area of the Great Falls International Airport. They were waiting for the arrival of Mitzi Quinata, Jay's mother-in-law, from Guam. While they waited, Jay and Rebecca reminisced about the time each of them had spent in Guam. Rebecca had worked two years as a librarian for Guam Christian Academy. During her second year as librarian, Jay had arrived on the island as an airman at Andersen Air Force Base.

"I'll never forget the day you introduced me to Angie," Jay said as his eyes remained glued on the runways in the distance. "If it hadn't been for you, I wouldn't be happily married and anxiously awaiting the birth of our first baby."

"That was a very interesting period in our lives," Rebecca replied. "Angie was the model student, and her mother was the best friend I had on the island. Most of the islanders kept their distance from statesiders, but Mitzi welcomed me with open arms and taught me the island ways," Rebecca said. "I'm so thankful we've been able to maintain our friendship through the years since I left Guam."

Jay nodded his head as he nervously watched the western sky. "I didn't expect Mitzi to fall in love with Montana the way she did when she was here for our wedding two years ago. Now that she'll soon have a grandbaby, it wouldn't surprise me if she moved to Montana after she retires from teaching."

"That would be nice," Rebecca agreed, "but people's roots run deep. When I was on Guam, I could hardly wait to get home. I'm sure she'll feel the same way when she's in Montana."

"There's one big difference," Jay teased. "Your true love was still in Montana while you were on Guam. They say true love knows no distance."

"I'll admit it was difficult making wedding plans while we were so far apart."

Simultaneously, they both rose to their feet as a faint speck appeared in the western sky. They stood in silence as the plane became larger, then finally touched down on the far runway. Jay and Rebecca watched as it taxied to the gate and the ramp was rolled out to the newly arrived plane. They waited as one by one the passengers deplaned.

After about a score of people emerged from the ramp, Jay spotted his mother-in-law and immediately ran to embrace her. "Welcome to Montana," he greeted. "How was your flight?"

"Long," Mitzi replied. "I was so afraid I wouldn't get here before the baby arrived that I couldn't sleep. I'll probably sleep all the way back to Rocky Bluff."

Mitzi then turned to Rebecca and hugged her. "Rebecca, I'm so glad you came to the airport with Jay. We have so much catching up to do. Guam Christian Academy just hasn't been the same since you left."

Rebecca grinned. "I hope the library automation system I installed is still working."

"Perfectly. It's the envy of all the other libraries on the island."

Mitzi turned her attention back to her son-in-law. "How's Angie?"

"She's doing great, but her boredom level is about maxed out," he laughed. "It's hard to keep a young, healthy woman flat on her back for over a month."

"I can imagine," Mitzi said with a chuckle

as the three walked toward the baggage claim area. "At least she made it, and the baby is big enough now that he or she won't be in any danger from low birth weight. Do you know if it's a boy or girl?"

Jay smiled and shook his head. "Everyone keeps asking us that, but we decided we didn't want to know until the baby is born. We'd rather be surprised."

"If it were me, I'd be dying of curiosity," Mitzi replied, then she shut her eyes and leaned her head back.

True to her word, Mitzi slept most of the way to Rocky Bluff. She awakened a few miles out of town and talked impassionately about her coming grandchild. Mitzi could hardly contain herself with excitement as Jay drove Rebecca to her home first.

As soon as Jay pulled into his driveway, Angie emerged from the front door to greet them. "What are you doing out of bed?" Mitzi scolded as she embraced her daughter.

"It's all right, Mother," Angie giggled. "Yesterday the doctor said I could be up and about. The baby is big enough and could come naturally any time." She heaved a deep sigh. "As far as I'm concerned, the sooner the better."

Angie and Mitzi walked into the house arm in arm, while Jay retrieved his mother-in-law's bags from the trunk of the car. The aroma of homemade bread filled the house. The table was set with their best china, topped off by a beautiful floral centerpiece.

Dawn Harkness appeared in the doorway of the kitchen. "Mitzi, it's so good to see you again," Dawn exclaimed as she hugged their newly arrived guest. "We thought you'd be hungry when you got in, so we fixed a ham with all the trimmings. I wanted to cook an old-fashioned Chamorro meal, but we couldn't find all the ingredients at the local grocery store."

"When I'm on Guam, I'll eat like a Chamorro, but when I'm in Montana, I'll eat like a Montanan," Mitzi laughed. "You shouldn't have gone to all this trouble."

"Yesterday when the doctor said I could be up and about again I just couldn't wait to get into the kitchen," Angie laughed. "Cooking has always been my least favorite thing to do, but when I had to depend on Dawn to do all the cooking, it suddenly became the thing I missed the most. Believe it or not, I've enjoyed spending the day in the kitchen."

"I really appreciate this," Mitzi replied. "Airplane food is so skimpy."

The savory meal was enriched by the delight the family shared in being reunited.

They made plans for the homecoming of the baby and shared the changes in Rocky Bluff since Mitzi had last been there two years before. Jay told Mitzi of his concern about his grandmother's health, then described the racial tension that had turned out to be the result of two traumatized boys.

Finally the conversation turned to the talk of the town. "Mom, do you remember Teresa Lennon, the director of the Spouse Abuse Shelter?" Angie asked.

"I didn't spend much time with her, but I was impressed with her compassion for other people. I was so grateful for the wise counsel she gave you," Mitzi said. "What's happening with her?"

"The first of June she's marrying our new pastor, Bryan Olson. The entire community is so excited."

Jay grinned and patted his wife on the shoulder. "The wedding is less than two weeks away, and Angie's afraid she'll be in the hospital and miss it."

"Mom, if I'm in the hospital on the big day, you'll have to go to the wedding in my place," Angie said as she laid her fork on her plate.

After the meal, Mitzi soon retired to the guest room, which Dawn had recently vacated. Mitzi slept the rest of the evening and throughout the entire night. Sleep was the only cure for jet lag.

The next week the Harkness family anxiously awaited the arrival of the baby. Mitzi helped plan the layette and shopped for baby necessities. A holiday atmosphere surrounded the Harkness household.

The evening of May thirty-first, Jay, Angie, and Mitzi were relaxing in the living room watching TV. Angie began to feel sharp abdominal pains. After the third one Mitzi said, "You better start timing those pains. Tonight could be the night."

"But they're not unbearable," Angie replied. "My friends tell me I don't have to worry until they get really bad."

"Trust me and begin timing them," her mother retorted.

The next pain came within five minutes. Jay hurried to the bedroom and grabbed the suitcase Angie had packed two days before. Mitzi wrapped her arm around her daughter as she escorted her to the car. In spite of her pain, Angie managed a shaky laugh. "It looks like I'm going to miss the big wedding after all," she quipped.

Ten o'clock the next morning, Edith was relaxing in the living room when the phone rang. She slowly walked to the kitchen phone. *Lately it takes too much energy to even walk the few feet to the telephone. My heart just doesn't seem to be able to keep enough blood pumping for me,* she thought as she reached for the phone.

"Hello?"

"Hello, Grandma. This is Jay. I have some exciting news for you."

Edith's face broke into a broad grin. "The baby must have arrived."

"How did you know?"

"Jay, I've known you all your life. Nothing would have made you this excited except a new baby. How are Angie and the baby doing? Is it a boy or girl? How much does it weigh? Have you named it yet?"

Jay shook his head. His grandmother had a knack of cutting right to the heart of a matter without mincing words. "To answer your questions in order," Jay laughed, "Angie and the baby are both doing great. It's a girl. And she weighs six pounds, nine ounces. We named her Edith Mae Harkness."

Edith froze, hardly comprehending what she had heard. "You mean you named her after me?" she said at last, her voice trembling. "Rocky Bluff now has a second Edith Harkness to carry on the tradition. I don't deserve such an honor."

"Grandma, we're honored to name her after you."

Edith shook her head in disbelief. "This is the second baby that has been named after me. Four years ago, Beth and Dan Blair named their baby Edith. But when they moved to Missoula, I never had a chance to get to know my little namesake." Edith paused. "But your baby will carry the Harkness name and will grow up right here in Rocky Bluff."

They talked some more about the baby; then Jay changed the subject. "Grandma, are you planning to go to the wedding this afternoon?"

"Oh yes," Edith replied enthusiastically. "I wouldn't miss this wedding for anything."

"Good," Jay replied. "I'll see you there. Angie's disappointed she won't be able to go, but her mother will stand in for her."

"I'm looking forward to seeing that new baby," Edith said as they ended their telephone conversation.

Edith slowly walked the few steps back to the recliner and sank deep into its cushions. *I have so much to be thankful for,* she mused as she thought back through the years. *I have a family that has been through a lot together and have grown strong in their love for God and each other. I spent many years trying to help the young people of Rocky Bluff, and I saw so many answers to prayer. I have truly been blessed with a full, worthwhile life, and I have lived to see my first great-grandchild. What more could I expect out of life? God has been so good to me.*

Teresa stood in the back of Rocky Bluff Community Church and surveyed the huge crowd that had gathered to help her and Bryan celebrate their wedding. A sweetness filled the church, as familiar hymns of love echoed from the organ. Beside her stood Andy Hatfield who was to escort her down the aisle. Since her own father had died several years before, she had chosen someone who had also experienced a midlife marriage to share these special moments.

As the organ music began to swell, Pastor Rhodes took his position in front of the altar. He was followed by Bryan, Bryan's brother who was best man, and the two Frank boys as junior groomsmen.

When the bridal march began, Teresa kept her eyes focused on Bryan as she walked slowly down the aisle. Her heart soared as she gazed upon her future husband. Bryan stood tall and handsome, dressed in a rented tuxedo. She had never seen him look so happy.

Bryan and Teresa repeated their wedding vows, their eyes fixed on each other. They had both heard the words hundreds of times before; only this time it was different. They were the ones making the pledges before God.

When Pastor Rhodes turned to Teresa and said, "Teresa Lennon, do you take this man, Bryan Olson, to be your lawful wedded husband?" Teresa's mind raced.

*I not only take Bryan as my husband, I accept his ministry as well. I will support his service to God in any way I can, whether it is in an active or a passive role.*

Somehow Bryan heard the words in Teresa's heart instead of the words on her lips. He whispered a "thank you" so softly that neither Pastor Rhodes nor the congregation heard or understood the intense spiritual commitment that was being made between the two.

Following the ceremony, Bryan and Teresa stood in the receiving line for an hour and a half, greeting well-wishers. When Jay Harkness and Mitzi Quinata came through the line, a puzzled expression, then a smile crossed Teresa's face. "Is Angie in the hospital?"

Jay nearly burst with pride. "Along with Edith Mae Harkness the Second, the most beautiful baby ever born in the Rocky Bluff hospital."

"Congratulations!" Teresa hugged the new father. "What did your grandmother say when you told her you had named the baby after her?"

"That was the first time I've ever heard her speechless," Jay chuckled. "I'd forgotten that Dan and Beth Blair had also named their second child after her. She couldn't believe that now two babies have been named after her."

Teresa nodded. "She's also had the new wing of the high school named after her. If anyone's life should be immortalized, it's hers."

Dawn Harkness was behind her brother in the receiving line. She too had a warm hug for Teresa. "Teresa, I want to wish you the very best. I'm leaving for college next week with a real purpose and mission. I don't know what I would have done without your compassionate understanding. If it wasn't for you and my family, I'm afraid to think about where I might be today."

Tears filled Teresa's eyes. Truly she felt as

committed to ministry as Bryan did, only in a different area of service. Because of her background, she reached out quickly to women in crisis. She glanced across the room at Michelle Frank who was surrounded by new friends. The nights of interrupted sleep and frustrations had been well worth the investment; she could see the changed lives around her.

Next the two Frank boys appeared in the receiving line. "Congratulations, Teresa. I hope you like living with the pastor as much as we did," they teased.

"I'm sure I will," Teresa smiled.

"Where are you going on your honeymoon?" Chuck giggled.

"That's a secret, but it's a long ways away," Teresa teased back.

"Are you going to leave tonight?" Chuck continued.

Teresa leaned over and whispered in his ear. "If you won't tell anyone, we have a honeymoon suite some place close by so we can rest for a couple days; then we're going to be some place no one can find us."

"Will you tell me where?" Chuck begged.

Hearing the young boy's plea, Pastor Olson leaned over. "Not on your life. I don't want to be awakened in the middle of the night." Everyone standing nearby burst into laughter.

The line seemed endless, but Teresa and Bryan enjoyed every minute of it. Teresa stepped out of her high-heeled shoes and hoped no one would notice her feet underneath her long wedding dress. The church had not been so packed in years. Everyone was bound together in a bond of love and well wishes.

At the very end of the reception line were Bob and Nancy Harkness, pushing Bob's mother in a wheelchair. Edith looked tired and worn, yet radiant.

Teresa bent over to give her a hug. "I'm so glad you could come and share this special time with us."

"I just had to be here," Edith replied. "I know how cautious I was in considering marriage later in life. But when I finally took the plunge, I cannot describe the happiness I had with Roy. I just wanted to wish you that same kind of happiness. I fully understand the lines in one of Robert Browning's poems that say, 'Grow old along with me! The best is yet to be.' "

# Chapter 15

The day after the wedding of Pastor Olson and Teresa Lennon, the Harkness family slept later than usual. When Nancy and Dawn went to the kitchen to prepare breakfast, Nancy glanced at the clock. "We'd better hurry," she said as she took a skillet out to begin frying eggs. "Pastor Rhodes is going to be preaching today, and we all want to welcome him back. Would you go check on your grandmother and see if she needs any help?"

Dawn smiled in agreement and hurried down the hallway. She knocked on the door. "Grandma? Grandma? Grandma, do you need any help?"

The room remained strangely silent. Dawn opened the door and peeked around the corner. Her grandmother remained perfectly still. She tiptoed toward the bed. "Grandma? Grandma?" There was still no response. Edith Dutton's eyes were closed, and a peaceful expression covered her face. Dawn took her hand. It was still and strangely cold. She turned and ran toward the door. "Mom! Dad! Come here quick! Hurry!"

Bob and Nancy came racing. They had not heard such urgency in their daughter's voice since she was a little girl. Inside his mother's bedroom, Bob instinctively took his mother's arm and felt for a pulse. His eyes widened, and he readjusted his fingers. Nothing. "I think she's gone," he said, his voice shaking. "We'd better call an ambulance."

Pastor Rhodes was immediately notified of the death of Edith Dutton. When he announced it to the congregation, gasps and faint sobs could be heard throughout the church. "Yes, this is a time of mourning. We all grieve the loss of a dear friend and community member," he said softly. Then he added confidently, "Yet this is also a time of rejoicing. Psalm 116, verse fifteen, says, 'Precious in the sight of the Lord is the death of His saints.' Edith was truly one of God's saints, and she is now released from her frail body to join our precious Lord and Savior in heaven. Let us all rejoice in her homegoing."

Word spread quickly of the death of Rocky Bluff's beloved Edith Harkness Dutton. The motels were crowded as friends and relatives gathered from all over Montana and neighboring states. Pastor and Mrs. Bryan Olson postponed their honeymoon to the Cayman Islands until after the funeral.

Pastor and Mrs. Rhodes remained in Rocky Bluff in order to officiate the service. At the request of the Harkness family, the funeral service would not be a time of eulogizing their mother and grandmother, but a time to express praise and thanksgiving to the Lord she served.

After the funeral, Edith Harkness Dutton was laid to rest in the Pine Hills Memorial Cemetery between her two husbands, George Harkness and Roy Dutton. The warm spring breeze whispering through the new leaves and the birds chirping in the trees seemed to say, "Welcome home, My beloved daughter. You have fought the good fight and have finished the race."

After the interment, the huge crowd in the church fellowship hall continued to reflect on the impact one woman's life had had on an entire community. Then one by one the congregation began to scatter to their own homes and motel rooms. The close friends and family were invited to an open house at the Harkness home for a special time of remembering.

The amount of food was overwhelming in the Harkness home during the open house, but few were interested in eating. Larry Reynolds stood to address the group. "I would like to share what a difference Edith Dutton made in my life," he began. "During the darkest day of my life, Edith was willing to risk her own life to prevent me from taking the life of my high school principal. She stood by me, believed in me until I could believe in myself and change my life."

Libby Reynolds, Larry's wife, nodded in agreement. "I found Roy and Edith Dutton's love for each other to be infectious. Through their example, Larry and I were able to rebuild a marriage that we felt was totally destroyed. I can truly say we experienced a type of contagious love."

Libby smiled across the room at Beth Blair who nodded knowingly. Many years ago they had shared troubled times together, and Edith Dutton had been there to act as their mentor. Beth could no longer hold back her words. "I want to emphasize what Libby said about how Roy and Edith Dutton's autumn love affected others. I met Edith when I came to Rocky Bluff as a scared, unwed teenage mother," she explained. "It was Edith's work at the crisis center that gave me the focus and direction I needed to take control of my life. It was Edith who upheld me with her prayers and encouragement during the days that my son Jeffey was kidnapped. It was Roy and Edith's love that inspired Dan and me. We discovered that we too could share a similar love because of the inspiration from the Duttons. Later we named our second daughter after Edith. You might say she was the one who inspired love between us."

Rebecca Hatfield nodded in agreement to Beth's words. "Beth was working with me at the Rocky Bluff High School when Jeffey was kidnapped. I don't know what we would have done without Edith during those dark days," Rebecca said. "When it came time for me to retire, I did not know what to do with myself. I assumed my productive years were over, but when I saw how Edith and Roy dedicated themselves to the crisis center, I realized I still had many productive years left to use my skills. I signed a two-year contract with a school on the island of Guam. I never thought that another chance at love would ever be possible, but because of Edith's example I found that distance could not be a hindrance for love. As soon as I returned from Guam, I followed Roy and Edith's example and began a beautiful marriage with Andy Hatfield. Ours was a distant love that grew into something close and permanent."

Angie Harkness remained seated on the sofa with her five-day-old baby on her lap. "I would like to add my thank you to all of you in this room," she began softly. "It was Rebecca who introduced me to Jay while he was stationed with the Air Force on Guam. When I too faced my darkest hour following a rape, I thought I was ruined for life and no respectable man would ever want to marry me. For me as well, it was Edith Dutton who brought renewal to my life so I could love again and later marry her grandson. Edith helped me find a healing love with Jay."

Bryan and Teresa Olson stood together holding hands. They were aglow with their new love. "I have known Edith for a long time," Teresa began. "We worked closely together when she was a counselor on the crisis line and I was director of the Spouse Abuse Shelter. Her compassionate love always served as a model for me. It was her love and encouragement that helped me accept and share my embarrassing, difficult background, and it was her wisdom and understanding that gave me the courage to follow my heart and marry Bryan Olson."

Bryan kissed his new bride on the forehead. "We will always be grateful for Edith's life. I came to Rocky Bluff as a confirmed bachelor, not knowing what real love was all about."

Bob Harkness stepped to the center of the room. "I'm grateful that each of you is sharing how Mother's love with Roy affected your life. I must admit that I nearly ruined it for all of you by resisting their marriage. Fortunately, our God of love is stronger than anything mortal man can do. I feel extremely blessed to have had a mother who had the compassion and wisdom to inspire all of our lives. We can truly say the world is a better place because Edith Harkness Dutton lived in Rocky Bluff, Montana."

A tiny whimper rose from within the blankets on Angie's lap. The young mother cuddled her new baby to her bosom. Jay looked on proudly. "We all have had so many experiences in which Grandma touched our lives. It was hard to say goodbye to her today, but her memory will always be with us. Every time I look at little Edith Mae Harkness, I will remember my responsibility to raise my daughter in love and faith. I want her to walk in the footsteps of the greatest woman that Rocky Bluff has ever known — Edith Harkness Dutton."

# ABOUT THE AUTHOR

**Ann Bell** is a librarian by profession and lives in Iowa with her husband, Jim, who is her biggest supporter. Ann has worked as a librarian and teacher in Iowa, Oregon, Guam, and Montana. She has been honored in the top three picks of *Heartsong Presents* members' favorite authors. Her eight *Heartsong* books all center around a fictional town in Montana called Rocky Bluff. She has also written numerous articles for Christian magazines and a book titled *Proving Yourself: A Study of James.*

The employees of Thorndike Press hope you have enjoyed this Large Print book. All our Thorndike and Wheeler Large Print titles are designed for easy reading, and all our books are made to last. Other Thorndike Press Large Print books are available at your library, through selected bookstores, or directly from us.

For information about titles, please call:
  (800) 223-1244

or visit our Web site at:
  www.gale.com/thorndike
  www.gale.com/wheeler

To share your comments, please write:
  Publisher
  Thorndike Press
  295 Kennedy Memorial Drive
  Waterville, ME 04901